The Decorating Club

A story about neighbors helping neighbors

Susan M. Meyers

Just Food For Thought, LLC

Fairfield, CT

Copyright © 2020 by Susan M. Meyers

All rights reserved. No part of this publication may be reproduced, distributed or transmitted in any form or by any means, without prior written permission.

For permission requests, write to the publisher, addressed "Attention: Permissions Coordinator," at the address below.

Just Food For Thought, LLC
P.O. Box 193
Fairfield, CT 06824

Library of Congress Control Number: 2020914170
Publisher's Note: This is a work of fiction. Names, characters, places, and incidents are a product of the author's imagination. Locales and public names are sometimes used for atmospheric purposes. Any resemblance to actual people, living or dead, or to businesses, companies, events, institutions, or locales is completely coincidental.

Cover design by Tugboat Design
Book Layout © 2017 BookDesignTemplates.com

The Decorating Club / Susan M. Meyers -- 1st edition
ISBN: 978-1-7337548-0-4 EBook
ISBN: 978-1-7337548-1-1 Paperback
ISBN: 978-1-7337548-2-8 Hardback

This book is lovingly dedicated
to Terry, who in every way is
that guy.

Contents

Acknowledgment 7

Preface 11

We're Moving? 21

Settled In? 33

The Decorating Club? 47

The Day After 57

House Rules 69

Your Style or Mine 79

Who Am I? 83

Purpose 95

Plan On It 113

Sharing the Load 125

Don't Settle 149

A New Day 159

Hard Hat Zone 177

Date Night 183

Be Courageous	187
Take 2?	205
The Gift Is in Giving	215
Navigating Change	233
Thankful Thursday	253
Life's a Celebration!	261
Personal Stick Figures	265
Forgiveness	271
Now What?	289
I'm Here...for Now	299
Afterword	315
Recipes	321
About the Author	325

Acknowledgment

While writing this book has been a long journey for me, I have always felt driven to move forward and complete it. Sure, at times, it was frustrating and emotionally challenging, but my strong desire to share the life message presented in the story and the encouragement of others fueled my determination.

Eventually, we all encounter trials that knock us down. Yet with them comes a choice: to either *give up* or *get up*. The sobering reality is that no one can do it for us. Yet I do believe there are angels among us, to help guide us in the right direction at just the right time. Those who without realizing it give us the hope and encouragement to carry on.

I found such a person in Tiffany Teichs.

Our first encounter came when I was wheeled into the physical therapy office where Tiffany worked. Right from the start, Tiffany made it clear that my injury was not going to heal all by itself and that I had to fight my own battle and take ownership. In addition to arming me with the necessary weapons and remaining by my side as I entered onto the battlefield, Tiffany also provided me with a safety net. It was a place where I could be weak and vulnerable on my road to rehabilitation. Then, at the appropriate time, with equal strength and kindness, she pulled away the safety net and pushed me back into life. Thank you, Tiffany!

I also give a special thank you to a man named Gary. I don't now recall his last name and have a feeling it doesn't really matter. Gary was there at one of those times when I was faltering and felt as though I was trapped in quicksand. He offered to say a prayer with me. His simple, caring act provided me the peace, courage, and commitment to continue moving forward.

Grace Haener, who, besides being my good friend, is one of the finest chefs I know. Grace, originally from India, continually expands upon her culinary talents by challenging herself to replicate cuisine from all around the globe. My very special thanks to Grace for allowing me to share her delicious recipe for Indian masala chai.

It is with fond appreciation that I also thank the original six members of the Decorating Club, all of whom hold a special place in my heart. We started out as neighbors and ended up becoming friends.

I am honored to be the mom of our four children—Chelsea, Terry II, Jillian, and Courtney—and am ever thankful for their unending love and support. Their belief in my ability is humbling.

It is true what they say: your life can change in the blink of an eye. It's easy to be there for loved ones when they are on top and independently living their lives, but when the blink occurs and their world comes crashing down, that's when true love comes into play.

I am eternally blessed to have a husband who continues to love and support me in every way. Terry is my biggest fan and the only person I know who would spend nearly an entire Hawaiian vacation in the shade editing one of the earlier versions that led to this book while the author sat poolside sipping piña coladas.

Above all, I thank the one who created me and to whom I owe my life. Thank you, Lord, for the gifts and talents you have given me and for always walking by my side and providing the love, patience, guidance, and strength to write this book."

Preface

Like a singer, I've been asked to write a love song
And fill it with whos, whats, wheres, and how longs
It should ring out in harmony about what I do best
With flowery words to complement and separate me from the rest
It should contain a roadmap to where my story will lead
And perhaps helpful background for others to get to know the real me
Well, as I struggled with my checklist and sought to satisfy
It suddenly occurred to me; It's not the what?
It's the why?

Why I wrote this book

I've been here before.

Have you ever felt that way? My guess is that most of us have at one time or another. Maybe that's why they say history repeats itself, if you don't learn from it.

Unfortunately for me, I didn't learn from my history, and as a result it came back to repeat—with a vengeance, taking me out at the knees figuratively and literally.

Let me explain.

It had all the makings of a perfect vacation. We were going to an island we loved and had been to many, many times before, but this time we were going by ourselves, without our four kids.

The weather in Aruba is always beautiful, and while there is a daily probability of rain, it usually occurs in the early morning and only lasts a few minutes.

With each of our children on somewhat of a steady course, the focus happily shifted to us: just a loving married couple with seven glorious days filled with sun, sand, and romance in their immediate future. At least that's what I was expecting.

In my mind, the vacation was also going to be somewhat of a reset for me, in an effort to reclaim my life. Mind you, it wasn't as if I felt I had actually lost my life; it was more that I had put a lot of it on hold and now wanted to start doing all the things I once enjoyed again, starting with tennis.

At check-in, I noticed that the resort was offering a free skills-sharpening clinic, so I signed myself right up and headed down to the court.

On the walk back, I was feeling pretty good about myself. After all, it had been years since I played tennis, and overall, I felt as though I had performed great during the clinic. I couldn't wait to tell Terry, and once I spotted him by the pool, I walked over, sat down, and filled him in on how well I had done. Several moments later, I went to stand but couldn't get up. It was if my back had locked into an unbreakable position and would neither bend nor move. Instantly, burning, stabbing pain radiated up and down my spine, and tears began to shoot from my eyes.

I spent the six remaining days of our vacation on my back marking time by Aruba's majestic sunrises and sunsets shadowed on the walls of our room. Upon arriving back home, I found myself dependent on loved ones for the everyday things I once took for granted.

It was clear; the life I had once known had come to a screeching halt!

Now with no guarantees on my future, I decided to pass on surgery and instead chose physical therapy. Thankfully, that placed me into the well-trained, strong, and kind hands of Tiffany. For the next several months, Tiffany worked closely with me, and together we focused all efforts on my rehabilitation.

* * *

"On a level of 1 to 10, with 10 being the worst, please tell me how bad your pain is; and on a level of 1 to 10 with 10 being the least, please tell me how much feeling you have in your leg; and on a level of 1 to 10, please tell me ..."

The barrage of questions continued, but the answer remained the same—10!

For me, the most pressing questions were, "How did I get here?" and "Where is here?" The last thing I remembered was being in Aruba on day one of my vacation.

* * *

My existence was no longer my own, and I longed for past days while torturing myself with the "what-if" game. What if I never went to Aruba; what if my back never heals; what if I never regain normal feeling in my leg; and what if ... ?

Fear, doubt, and self-pity had entered and showed no sign of leaving anytime soon. I tried convincing myself that if I could just have my old life back again everything would be great. However, I soon came to realize that I didn't want my old life back, because everything wasn't great.

Somewhere along the line, I had stopped being me. I couldn't point to an exact start date or even a specific reason; it was more a combination of things, sort of a cumulative effect.

For example, the kids were getting older and were no longer under our watchful eyes. That left a lot of room for me to worry. Eventually I became obsessed with their safety. Were they making the right choices? Were they eating right? Were they getting sick again? And so on.

I also began to settle. I know we all get older and no one stays the same, but the sobering realization hit me hard. It happened one morning after rubbing the sand out of my eyes and stumbling to the sink to brush my teeth. As I glanced up, I saw the reflection of a woman I no longer recognized. Sure, I knew it was me, but it was not really me!

The once daily, full-of-life spark that gleamed from my eyes was missing. I had begun to feel as if I no longer served a purpose and just moved through my days always expecting a problem. As a result, I was close to giving up trying.

* * *

"So, Susan, how do you feel today?" said Tiffany cheerfully. "On a level of 1 to 10, with 10 being the worst, please tell me how bad your pain is. And on a level of 1 to 10..."

"Stop!" I shouted, interrupting Tiffany midsentence. "Do you have a plus 10 on your scale?" I snapped. I was in pain mentally and physically, and I didn't care who knew it.

* * *

Just when I felt things were at their worst, one day I heard a small voice whisper, "Food for thought." My eyes quickly looked around the bedroom, yet no one was there. In the days and weeks to come, the voice frequently returned repeating the same three words: "Food for thought." I was the only one who heard the voice, and there was no reasonable explanation as to why. "Well, that's it; I'm losing my mind now too!" I thought.

Even so, something seemed familiar to me, almost as if I had felt this way before.

Then all of a sudden, it came back to me: I had been here before. It was a place filled with worry, doubt, and fear. It was a time when self-pity got the best of me. Another time in my life when "me" was not really "me," and life as I knew it was on hold.

Then entered the Decorating Club, and along with it came an opportunity for me to serve others. In an instant my life changed; I had been called upon to do the things

I did well and personal happiness and gratitude soon followed.

Inspired by true-life experiences, the story of the Decorating Club is a simple tale of neighbors helping neighbors. It is not a how-to on mixing florals and stripes, nor does it reveal a multistep program for achieving success. Rather, the story focuses on the exploits of an eclectic group of women who suddenly find themselves with rooms that no longer serve a purpose and an opportunity to make a change. It describes their personal journeys of growth resulting from having come together.

While most of the women have no prior experience, all agree to step out of their comfort zone, roll up their sleeves, and try. With each home comes a new story and a focus seamlessly shifting back and forth between applying paint or incorporating fabric and sharing and supporting each other through the various challenges of life. The end result is a selection of personalized homes, "professionally" designed by the women who live in them and what offers to become a contagious example for others.

Importantly, in real life, not all of the members opted for their own project, and some even relocated before having the opportunity. Nonetheless, all were strongly committed to the spirit of helping each other. It was a very rewarding experience for me, and although we have since lost touch, I would like to think for each of the other members. Perhaps standing outside looking in, one might clearly have seen there was more to it than just redesigning homes.

For me, recalling those times reminded me of the importance of never giving up and never giving in on being the person I was made to be.

It is my sincere hope that the story will both inspire and motivate you to ask yourself, on a level of 1 to 10 with 10 being the *best*, are you living the life you were made to live?

Just food for thought,

Susan M. Meyers

THE DECORATING CLUB

Where did that person go?

While cleaning out your attic you come across a box. It's packed with old pictures and time-dated mementos. You get comfortable on the floor and randomly start pulling out its contents in search of clues as to the meaning of the container and the identity of all the faces in the photos. You find matchbook covers with names of restaurants adorned in fancy gold script, first-place ribbons and championship trophies, old musty blue-and-gold soccer socks and photos of people around cakes, in front of Christmas trees, and dressed in gowns and tuxedos. You discover papers handwritten with poems, cheering chants and little diaries with no keys.

There are broken necklace chains and tarnished promise rings. Some newspaper clippings of a football upset; announcements of wedding proposals and the help wanted section with big red circles around several of the ads.

As you keep digging, you glance past concert ticket stubs and car loan payment books and then suddenly you find something official looking...it's a social security card with a youthful signature scribbled on the front, and just above that, neatly typed, is the name you were given at birth.

All of a sudden, it comes back to you: this is no ordinary box, it's a time capsule of your life buried deep within the interior of your home.

As your mind races to recapture the lived moments portrayed through the collection of mementos, you can't help but wonder, where did that person go?

CHAPTER 1

We're Moving?

"BECAUSE IT was like the Lord whispered in our ears and told us it's time to go."

That was Sarah's answer to everyone who asked why she, Tommy and their four children along with their dog Sadie would just pack up and move. It left everyone they knew scratching their heads as they tried to understand why a successful, well-liked couple surrounded by friends and family would just throw caution to the wind and start completely over—and why would they pick a state where they knew no one and was hours away from their home?

Although Tommy, the older of two sons, was raised in Queens, NY, with his family, career-wise he had "grown up on Wall Street" and was now a consultant to financial services companies.

Sarah, the youngest of three, lived in northern New Jersey with her parents, brother and sister.

Shortly after she and Tommy married, the couple moved to Ridgewood, NJ, approximately forty-five minutes away from where she grew up. Both Sarah and Tommy loved the area and felt that it was the perfect place to raise their family.

Tommy enjoyed a comfortable commute to work each day into New York City. Sarah, on the other hand, owned a creative design business and worked out of their home.

With four little ones, all close in age, life was anything but boring.

The decision to move came during the spring of 2001. It started when Tommy returned home after spending the day in Connecticut, visiting with a client. During his several-hour drive back home he had the opportunity for some rare "quiet time" and was moved to consider things he hadn't before. As a result, by the time he got home, Tommy was anxious to ask Sarah a very important question.

"Mom, Mom, Sadie pooped in the living room again," said Maddie "...and ohhh that's so gross, Katie just stepped in it!"

"What?? Oh great!! Get her outside right now Maddie!" shouted Sarah from upstairs.

"Katie?" asked Maddie.

Sarah quickly put the toilet brush back into its holder and ran into the hallway,

"No! Take Sadie outside, Maddie!"!" she scolded.

"Mommmm, the phone was ringing in your office and I accidently picked it up. It's some lady named Mrs. Gorilla and she says she wants to talk to you, NOW!" said Darcy.

"Mrs. Gorilla? Oh no, you mean Mrs. Purrella?"

"Yeah, I guess but well, I mean she sounds like a big mean ape anyway."

"Darcy, Shhh!! Be quiet!! ...and how many times have I told you not to answer my phone?"

"I know but it was an accident, sorry."

Tommy pushed the button for the remote and then carefully drove the car into the garage.

Once inside, he gathered up his lose papers, grabbed his BlackBerry and briefcase and headed inside the house through the kitchen door.

"Hey Dad how was your day?"

"It was good Collin, but yours isn't going to be if your mother sees you drinking from the milk carton again."

"Yikes, your right! But don't tell her Dad 'cause she's already on the path," he pleaded.

"What path?"

"You know the one you always say when somebody is mad."

"Oh, you mean warpath."

"Yup, that's the one!"

Tommy left the kitchen and walked over to the bottom of the staircase.

"Hey Sarah, I'm home. Are you up there?"

"No, I'm over here," said Sarah as she closed the door to her office and met up with Tommy near the dining room entrance.

"How was your day?" asked Tommy.

"It was ok, how was yours?"

"It was g-r-e-a-t!

In fact, I want to talk to you about an idea I have. Let's sit down over here."

Tommy pulled out one of the upholstered chairs for Sarah to sit on and positioned another right next to her for himself.

"That's just perfect," moaned Sarah.

"What?" asked Tommy.

"Don't you see this big stain on this chair?" she asked impatiently.

"Oh, don't worry about it Sarah, I'm sure it will come out."

"No it's not going to come out and this fabric was very expensive!

It seems like we just can't have anything nice anymore, everything always has to get ruined."

"Come on honey, don't worry about it I'm sure it will be alright and if it doesn't come out just have a new one made."

"It doesn't work that way Tommy, I can't even get the fabric anymore," she sighed.

Tommy put his arm around Sarah and said, "Listen, on the way home an idea popped into my head and I want to talk to you about it."

"Okay, what's the idea?"

"Well, I was thinking maybe we should move."

"Move?! Move to where?"

"I don't know. We'll have to figure that part out. I first wanted to make sure it would be something you'd be open to."

"Wow! I wasn't expecting that to be the first thing you said when you got home. Are you serious, or are you joking around like when you told me you wanted to raise goats?"

"Well for the record I was only part teasing with you then. I still think there's a lot of perks to raising goats. You know, like we could make our own goat cheese." Tommy laughed.

"You're impossible!"

I know, but this time I am serious. Honestly, it's given me a peaceful feeling just thinking about it. But what do you think? Would you be open to the idea of moving?"

Sarah sat quietly for a moment as she stroked her chin with her right thumb and index finger then she said, "Well, to be completely honest, lately I have been daydreaming about the possibility of us one day living somewhere else.

"Kinda like a fresh new start and I for one could use that right about now."

"So yeah, I guess I would. I mean, I don't know where we'd go, and of course, I'd still want to make sure we could come back and visit Mom, Dad, and everybody else. But to be honest, it is kind of exciting to think about moving. I really feel like I could use a change. But how would we do it? I mean, what about your job, and my business? Plus, we'd have the house to deal with and of course the kids with school."

"Well, I was thinking I'd talk to my boss first and see if I could transfer to another location. Then at least I could still stay with the company and we wouldn't have to start completely over. Although, the way I feel right now, if need be I'd be up for that too, as long as you were by my side."

"Wait, you mean with another company?"

"Yeah, why not?"

"Well, you've been with them a long time. What if you can't get another job?"

"Yes, but we won't know unless we try, and besides, what if I got a better job?"

"Ok, but, you do realize everyone will think we're nuts, right?"

"I don't care what everyone else thinks. All I know is that I have a strong feeling as if we are being told to move. The fact that you were having a similar thought makes it even more obvious that the crazier thing would be if we didn't listen."

"Yeah, that is strange that we've both separately been having the same thought," admitted Sarah.

"Yes but I'm confused what did you mean by a fresh start and why didn't you say anything sooner?" asked Tommy.

"I guess I didn't say anything because I thought it would be impossible for us to just pick up and move. As for the way I'm feeling, I guess it's a combination of things." Sarah's eyes filled with tears.

"What's the matter, honey? Why are you crying?"

"I don't know. I know I should be happy and I want to be happy but for some reason I'm just not. I just don't feel like myself anymore."

"Is it me? Have I done something?"

"No, of course not, I love you."

"I know you love me, but we both know I can be a bit of a handful at times," Tommy said jokingly. "Is anything up with the kids that you're concerned about?"

"No, I mean just the regular stuff, but that's not causing me to feel this way—they're great. I don't know, Tommy, I just don't know. Although I'm sure work probably is part of it."

"What do you mean? You've always told me how much you enjoy it."

"Well I do, but lately it's becoming less fun, and well, secretly I've been wondering how much longer I would want to do it anyway."

"Why?"

"Why? Umm, okay, I'll give you an example. Remember me telling you about Mrs. Princeton?"

"Yes, aren't you redoing her family room?"

"That's right. Well, yesterday morning she called me up crying hysterically."

"Wow, was she really crying? What happened?"

"Yes! She told me that she thought Rafael used two different colored paints while painting her family room because the walls didn't look the same color. I told her that he was a professional who has been in business for over thirty years and I strongly doubted he would have made such a mistake, but happily offered to come by and take a look."

"Well, that's good. What did she say?"

"She asked me if he had a drinking problem!"

"What?"

"I know! So, okay, I went over to her house later in the day, and the paint was exactly the same."

"Then why did she think it was different?"

"Turns out, when she called me yesterday morning the sunshine from her skylight was casting a shadow onto one of the adjacent walls. Yet when I went there yesterday afternoon the sun had moved and the wall without the shadow was exactly the same as the other walls."

"Oh my gosh, that's funny. But is she happy now?"

"No! Now she's questioning the fabric used for the window treatments."

"But I thought you said she loved it."

"She originally did! However, it's the one her sister-in-law picked out. She passed on the one I suggested, but now she thinks her sister-in-law didn't have her best interests at heart and told me I should have stopped her from picking it!"

"Oh boy!"

"Exactly! And that's just one client! Most of them are the complete opposite."

"Well, I guess that's good. I mean if they aren't as extreme as Mrs. Princeton, it must be a lot easier, right?"

"Wrong. Instead they're too busy and don't have any time to tell me what they want—they just tell me to do what I like or whatever's trendy."

"Oh, and I can see how that wouldn't work with you—your whole business is based on helping people create a home that reflects them and not you."

"Exactly!"

* * *

The very next morning Tommy approached his boss and spoke to him about the possibility of relocating within the company.

"Gee Tom; this comes as a big surprise. Why the heck do you want to move? Is everything alright with the family?"

"Yes, Ed everyone is fine. Sarah and I just felt like we wanted a change. We figured if we were going to make a move now would be the perfect time – especially while the kids are still young," said Tommy.

"Well I get that Tom, and appreciate your desire to stay with the company; after all you've been here a long time. But, right now, the only possibility I can see is if we moved you over to central Atlantic – and I have to be honest with you, you'd have to reinvent yourself and create a whole new book of business. I'd also still need you to make frequent trips back here to take care of your current clients until I got someone to pick up the slack. Are you sure that's something you'd want to do?" asked Ed.

As soon as Tommy finished talking to his boss and ironing out the possible logistics he picked up the phone and dialed Sarah.

"Hello," said Sarah into the phone.

"Hi Sarah, well I've got some good news and some bad news. What would you like to hear first?" asked Tommy.

"Give me the good news first!" demanded Sarah.

"Well, Ed said they'll support me in our desire to relocate but the bad news is Tahiti is out," laughed Tommy.

"Tahiti? I didn't say it had to be Tahiti, although that would be amazing!" said Sarah.

"I know I'm just teasing but you've always told me how romantic it would be to go there," said Tommy.

"Yes but maybe for an anniversary not to live there," said Sarah.

"Ok in that case I've got nothing but good news," laughed Tommy.

CHAPTER 2

Settled In?

IN LATE AUGUST the family of six set off from their home in northern New Jersey to begin the next chapter of their lives in Crofton, Maryland, a relatively quiet "bedroom community." It was located just outside the Washington beltway and close to Annapolis.

Sarah and Tommy's new home was on a cul-de-sac off Meadowbrook lane. The neighborhood was comprised of a mixture of business owners, executives and contractors as well as a large number of secret service and other government employees. Their real estate agent had explained that due to its proximity to Washington, DC, and the natural cycles that occurred following each election period, the neighborhood turned over faster than other areas.

It wasn't long before the family was beginning to settle into their new routines. The kids began school with the two oldest attending Crofton Middle and their two younger siblings at Crofton Elementary.

Although they weren't excited about starting the school year earlier than back home, they were enjoying making new friends.

Tommy was becoming a pro at battling the beltway and building his business relations throughout the areas of Maryland, Virginia and Washington, DC, and Sarah was even starting to think about possibly restarting her business, perhaps taking a new approach this time. Everything was seemingly moving forward as planned.

Then, a few weeks later, on a bright and sunny Monday in September, the world stopped spinning: as if a switch had just been flipped.

Sarah and Tommy, along with the rest of the world watched in horror as the burning towers were played out repeatedly on every channel.

The promise and excitement of a new start had now been replaced with sadness, loneliness and fear of what might come next.

Now with one foot in Maryland, where they knew hardly anyone and the other back home in New Jersey, their hearts ached as they tried to get their heads around the question everyone was struggling with—why?

* * *

... "No, Tommy's fine and the kids are all okay, I guess. I mean they're just very confused though. It's nonstop all over the TV day and night. It's hard to escape it, and I'm sure that's what's causing their nightmares. What's it like back home? Is everybody okay?"

... "Me?" Sarah stopped, shaken for a moment as she tried to gain control of herself. " ... I'm okay I guess."

... "No, I haven't really met anyone, and I really don't want to right now."

... "I don't know; I just don't feel like it!"

... "Yes, I know I was looking forward to a fresh new start, but I wasn't expecting it to turn out like this! On top of it, Kara, I'm really worried about Mommy, and I feel extremely helpless being here while she's so sick. Do you think she's going to be alright?"

... "Yes. Yeah, I understand."

... "What? No, I haven't started decorating the house yet! Because I don't feel like it!"

... "Well, not much. I watch the stupid news and then wait for Tommy and the kids to come home; that's basically it."

... "I don't know, Kara. It's hard to put the way I feel into words, but I guess some days I wake up questioning my life."

... "No, not Tommy and the kids, just the 'me' part of my life. I mean, don't you ever wonder if there's more than just Meatless Monday and Taco Tuesday? For me, it's as if I get up and just hit the reset button. I keep asking myself whether there's more or if this is all there is? I mean, really what purpose, if any, do I serve?"

... "I know, I know! But I mean beyond being a wife and mother. That part of my life is good. I'm not talking about that!"

***

Volunteer?

You decide to do some volunteer work reasoning that so many people are doing it and besides it's the right thing to do. So you join your church on an outing to go feed the homeless, but after stealing a piece of chicken off one of the plates, you're asked to leave and not return. Next, you join a bunch of friends in volunteering at a local hospital, but at the first sign of blood, you awake to them picking you up off the floor. Totally embarrassed you vow never to step foot in a hospital again.

While opportunities continue to come and go, none seems to be a perfect fit. Until all of a sudden, you get a desperate call from a committee leader begging you to join a small group on a sojourn to the state prison. It seems there was an outreach for participants to join in meeting the unfulfilled need for visiting convicts on death row.

When you arrive, you are introduced to inmate #6783, who you find to be a seemingly kind, quiet and reserved elderly woman named Mary, and not at all what you were expecting. You try to look past what she's accused of and focus on who she is now: a gentile woman with no family, friends or any soul in the world who cares about her.

Eager to catch up on lost time, Mary proclaims her decision to adopt you. She demands that you fill her in on everything she's missed from one birthday to the next.

"Please," she cries, "I want to be a proud momma before I die. I need you to brag to me about all the things you've accomplished in life so far, and don't break my heart by telling me you can't think of any."

Then in rapid fire, your newly adoptive momma instructs you to start by telling her about the quiet, untold acts of kindness you performed when no one was looking.

Next, she asks you to speak about your talents; things you've had interest in and continually worked on to improve.

Then she asks you for your list of gifts; those bestowed upon you, the things only you were born to do.

Followed quickly by, "Tell me the stories of how you've used your gifts and talents to touch the lives of others."

Finally, she asks you to speak of your proudest moment and fill her in on what you do better than anyone else in the world.

Astonished and sitting there in silence, you think to yourself, "What am I going to say?"

* * *

It wasn't long after speaking with her sister that one of Sarah's greatest fears became a reality.

"Oh, Mom, I really miss you. You're my best friend. You've always known just what to say and, boy, I could really use that right now! I'm so unhappy and scared!—and it didn't help that you had to go and die on me!" Sarah said through her sniffles.

Looking at the clock and realizing it was almost time for the school bus to arrive, she grabbed her keys and headed for the door. As she slid the key into the lock, Sarah had a thought, "Hmmm, maybe I should move forward and restart my design business after all. At least that would get me off the couch."

Sarah opened the door to the family minivan and then quickly closed it.

"I think I'll walk to the bus stop today. God knows I could definitely use the exercise."

Walking to the top of her street Sarah then made a right onto Meadowbrook. The day was warm and sunny, and it took only a few minutes before Sarah was wiping the sweat off her forehead.

"Well if Kathleen is right, that is one thing I'm going to be happy about this winter." Tommy and Sarah's real estate agent had told them that they could expect the average temperatures to run approximately ten to twelve degrees warmer than what they were used to back in New

Jersey. That would be a welcomed relief for Sarah, who had always hated winter's chill.

"Oh my gosh, what in the world is that, and how did I not notice it before?"

As Sarah approached the bus stop, she noticed a pink-colored house on the corner, trimmed in black and accented by a bright green painted front door. "Wow that looks like a watermelon. I wonder who lives there. Better yet, I wonder what the inside looks like!" Suddenly Sarah raised her right hand and began scratching the back of her neck. It was something Tommy pointed out that she did every time she got nervous.

"Oh Lord, I really don't know if I'm up for that again! Some of my clients were sooo challenging and I'm already tired just thinking about them! Ugh, not to mention what it would take to become established again. I'd have to get business cards, open a bank account, register with the state, obtain insurance, make all new connections and... No!" Sarah folded her arms across her chest and began shaking her head from left to right throwing her short blonde hair into the air like a whirlybird yard decoration. "I can't... I can't!"

Sarah spent the next several moments trying to convince herself that restarting her business was a bad idea.

"After all, the couch is kind of comfy and besides I haven't even decorated my own home.

"It's been a while since I've worked on a design project. In fact, I'm not sure I even have what it takes anymore.

"Oh suck it up Sarah, that's nonsense. Of course I do, I'm a great designer. I'm great at many things. The problem is I'm just not doing any of them.

"That's what's wrong I've put my life on hold; instead, I need to get out there and live it. My problem is I've been spending too much time thinking and not enough time doing.

"Hmm, what was it she used to say? Oh, that's right: 'Sarah if you don't use it, you'll lose it!'

Thanks for the lightbulb moment Mom."

* * *

Later that evening over dinner, Tommy cautiously approached Sarah with an idea. "Hey, I was thinking and have something I want to bounce off you. What do you think about restarting your business here in Maryland now that we're settled in?"

Staring at him in shock, Sarah responded, "Wow you must be a mind reader? I just started thinking the same thing. I mean, you know, in the future, but not right this minute. I'm not ready right now. Maybe after we're all settled in. Besides, I can't start another design business when my own home isn't even done.

"Plus, the people around here have never even heard of me or my business. That's something that's going to take time to build up again!"

"So I guess it was a bad idea. I'm sorry I asked," Tommy replied. "But then again, if I heard you right, you said you're just 'not ready.' Is that true?"

"Yeah, I guess that's right," Sarah replied hesitantly.

"Okay, I get that. I also know that's never stopped you before from doing something you wanted to do. You never give up until you figure it out. So my question for you is what are you going to do to get ready?" Tommy asked.

"Hmm, you're right, Tommy. I guess I've just been making a lot of excuses, but it is still scary, and I'm nervous," said Sarah.

"I understand, but you have too much to offer. I think you just need to start. And as far as our house goes, well, I'm thinking you already have your first new client waiting for you," said Tommy.

Sarah smirked.

"Well, I guess it's time I get started, then. After all, I don't want to keep them waiting!" She chuckled to herself.

THE DECORATING CLUB

* * *

Over the next few weeks, Sarah was busy creating storyboards for each one of the rooms in their home. Many of them based on past memories and included places and activities their family had enjoyed.

As Sarah sat daydreaming an idea for the last room popped into her mind. "Oh, I have the perfect theme for our family room. Tommy and the kids are going to love it!" Then Sarah started to laugh. "Oh my gosh, he was crazy! He was so determined to catch that darn fish. I can hear him now: 'Just a little longer, honey. I can see him following the lure!' It didn't matter that it was pouring out and I was stuck in the rental car with four little kids and one just happened to be throwing up!"

The next day, with the creation of all the boards behind her, Sarah immediately got to work on what she dubbed 'the fun part'. Each day shortly after Tommy left for work and the children were all on board the bus, Sarah jumped into her painting clothes, filled her extra-large mug full of coffee and headed up her ladder, remaining until the end of the day when her family returned back home.

"Hey, Mom, I'm home. Where are you?"

"I'm upstairs, Collin."

Leaping up two stairs at a time, Collin quickly reached the top floor. "Oh wow, Mom, this is beautiful! Does Darcy know you're painting seashells on her wall?"

Pointing to the wall over Darcy's bed, Sarah explained, "Well she doesn't know I'm painting this seashell swag, but she does know I'm painting the walls to look like faux whitewashed paneling. Do you think she'll like it?"

"Oh yeah, I think this looks great. She's going to love it! Mom, you're doing such a great job. I mean the whole house looks awesome."

Sarah put down the paintbrush and climbed down off the ladder to inspect her work. "Ouch! Looks like I'm a bit stiffer than I thought."

"What's the matter, Mom? Are you okay?" asked Collin.

"Yes, honey, I'm fine. I think my body is just trying to get my attention and tell me it wants a little break."

"Well you should take a break. You've been working all day for like forever on the house. Besides, Kyle's mother said she saw you up really high on the ladder and you looked like you were going to fall, and I don't want anything to happen to you, Mom, because . . ."

"Wait, what did you say? Kyle who? And when did she see me on my ladder?"

"Oh, Kyle Scheck. They live at the top of the community up by the bus stop. I overheard her talking to some of the other moms. They were calling you the 'new neighbor who moved in but never came out,' and they were all laughing saying, 'I wonder if she really even exists.'"

"What!"

"No, but it's okay, Mom, 'cause Kyle's mom stood up for you."

"And how did she do that, Collin?"

"She said you do exist because she's seen you."

"When did she see me?"

"Oh, she said she's come by a couple of times and looked in the windows."

Sarah smiled to herself. "Hmm, so I guess they have heard of me after all."

CHAPTER 3

The Decorating Club?

"MOM, WHAT are you doing?" asked Daniella.

"I'm waiting for this woman to pull out of the spot," answered Maggie.

"But there's a ton of spots down there. Just take one of those."

"I know, honey, but this one's close to the entrance. Let's just give her another minute."

"Oh, give me a break. So we walk a little further. I don't have all day. I need to get my homework done; I'm going out later with my friends. Besides, she's never going to move. She knows you're waiting for the spot. Come on, just park somewhere else!" demanded Daniella.

Maggie took her foot off the brake and coasted down to the next available space. After putting the car in park and turning off the motor, she firmly grasped the steering wheel and shifted her weight up and out of the driver's seat. "Okay, dear, I know you'll be in the shampoo aisle, but if you get done before me I'll be over in the baking section," volunteered Maggie.

"What a surprise," snapped Daniella.

The pair got out of the car and headed inside the store. Once inside, they went their separate ways, with Daniella making a beeline to the personal care section, while Maggie headed over to the baking aisle.

Once there, Maggie lifted a bag of flour from the shelf, turned, and placed it into her cart.

"Oh hi, Maggie. I was wondering if that was you," said the woman standing right behind her.

"Hey, Carol, how are you?"

"I'm good, thanks. Oh, by the way, I love your new vinyl fence. It looks really good. Darnell and I are thinking of putting one up between us and the Thompkins." Nervously looking to the right and left she then whispered, "Because I can't stand their dog always coming over doing his business on our lawn."

"I understand," said Maggie sympathetically.

"By the way, have you met the new neighbors who moved into the Murphy's house yet?" asked Carol.

"No, I haven't, although I have seen the kids around. I know there's four of them," answered Maggie.

"Yes, that's right; they have three girls and one boy. I've met the boy. His name is Collin. A very nice young man. He came to my door selling popcorn for the Scouts. He told me he has a twin sister named Maddie, they're the oldest, then a sister named Darcy, and the youngest I believe is Katie.

"Darnell told me he met the dad. His name is Tommy. I think he told me he saw him at Lowes or Home Depot. Anyway, he went right up to him and introduced himself. That's my Darnell, Mr. Outgoing," she said smiling. "Hey, did you receive an invitation to go to their house for a party? I hear the whole community is invited—well at least the women, that is."

"Yes, I did get an invitation. I thought they were so cute. I mean who thinks of sending out hardboiled eggs in brown paper bags as an invitation?" said Maggie.

"I know, how clever. It must have taken a long time to glue all the yellow fun fur and googly eyes onto all those eggs. Yet very creative and appropriate for a Chick's Night theme. I think it's kind of strange that nobody's ever met the mom yet, though. The little boy told me his grandma died and he overheard her saying she didn't want to talk to anybody. Instead, she's just been working on their house. He said she's some kind of designer.

"Personally I thought the house looked beautiful the way Darlene and Jeff had it. I can't imagine what she's been doing with it for the last eight months, but I guess we'll all get to see very soon!"

* * *

With the longest driveway in the community, Sarah and Tommy's home had previously enjoyed the reputation of being "the party house," and all Sarah's invitees were pleased to see that the newbies appeared to be continuing that tradition.

When the big night finally arrived, the house was filled to the brim with "chicks" of all shapes and sizes, each looking to have a good time. Most of the crowd had been to the house many times before and were eager to peek at Sarah's redesign so they could compare, comment and, of course, report back to the previous owners.

The community was just over five years old and almost all of the homes there still had the white walls provided by the builder. So it came as no surprise to Sarah that there was a fair amount of chirping about her bold use of color and creative themes.

When asked, Sarah shared her belief that every home should tell a story of those who live there and that she had made a successful, albeit at times frustrating career helping her clients tell their own story. Regardless of whether it was for a home or a business, Sarah always used the same approach.

First, Sarah would help them identify *where they were in their vision*; next, she would help them determine exactly *where they wanted to go*, and finally, she would tie it all together by collaborating with them to develop a personalized plan for *how they were going to get there*.

The women now were seeing just a small part of Sarah and Tommy's story.

"Where did you get those lovely curtains?" asked Mary Jo, an elderly neighbor who lived right next door.

Sarah smiled coyly, and then said, "Oh, we made them. Tommy crafted them from wood, and I painted them."

"Wood? But they look like real fabric," chimed in another woman.

"Thanks, that's what I was hoping for. It's actually a style of painting known as trompe l'oeil, where it's intended to trick the eye and in this case give the illusion of being a curtain made from pleated fabric."

"Well, you sure tricked me!" Mary Jo remarked.

Sarah simply smiled, but inside her mind, she was vividly replaying a past moment in time.

> "Sarah, look at this combination. I did a pattern with yellow, white and blue. What do you think?" her mom said as she proudly stood to show off her handiwork. Just then, all the beads slipped off the wire, bouncing in every direction. "Oh no, not

again!" they both screamed, followed by a joyous laughter that Sarah would never forget.

With every room came another story and another expression of the passions shared by the couple and their four children.

"Hey, somebody take a picture of me!" yelled out one of the women as she wrapped her arms around one of the life-sized stuffed bears positioned next to the fireplace.

"This room is incredible, Sarah, it looks just like a lodge I once stayed in out West. I can't believe there's real logs on the ceiling and walls. Did you have someone do that for you?" asked one of the neighbors.

"My husband, Tommy, did it," said Sarah proudly. "We actually ordered the logs from a company in Michigan, and they delivered them right to our driveway."

"What about the furniture, did your husband make it as well?" asked another woman.

"No," laughed Sarah. "It is made out of real logs, though, but we went down to Furnitureland South and ordered it."

"Where's that, Sarah? I never heard of it."

"Furnitureland South is in High Point, North Carolina. It's the world's largest furniture store."

"Did you say in the world?" questioned another one of the women.

"Yes, they have over 1.3 million square feet. Trust me, you would love it!" exclaimed Sarah.

"You guys have to check out the upstairs bathroom. It's painted to look like a library with shelves and shelves of books."

"My favorite is the French country kitchen. Did you see the chicken painted on the wall and then covered with barbed wire and wood? It looks like a real chicken coop!"

"Oh yeah, I like that too, but did you notice the artificial rooster posed at the top of it? When I walked past I saw its feathers move, and I was like WHAT? I had to look again to see if I was seeing things!"

"Did anybody go in the guest room downstairs? It's made up to be like a country inn."

"Boy, she's amazing. It's unbelievable what she's done with the house."

"Yes, she's very talented. I wish I had a little of that talent."

"Well you know it's what she does for a living."

"Oh, I didn't know that!"

"Yes, I heard she had a business in New Jersey."

"Cool, do you think she's going to restart it down here? I would love for her to come over to my house."

"I don't know, but that would be great. I'd have her at my house too."

"Yeah, me too!"

"Me too!"

"I would too!"

"Hey, Sarah, a bunch of us are wondering if you are going to restart your business here in Maryland. We'd love for you to work on our homes."

Sarah nervously began to scratch the back of her neck. She had not anticipated the question, and it left her speechless for a few seconds. Sarah felt that she was still not quite ready to take on the commitment of restarting her business—at least not at that moment. Thinking quickly, and hearing her mom's words run through her mind again—"Use it or you'll lose it," she suggested a possible alternative.

"Umm, no, I'm not, but I'll make you a deal. If you're all willing to try, agree to roll up your sleeves and promise to work together alongside me, I'll be happy to help you."

The enthusiastic group of six women excitedly agreed without hesitation, and that night with Sarah as their guide formed the Decorating Club, with the express intention of "turning houses into homes one room at a time."

* * *

"So how'd your Chicks' Night go?" Tommy asked when he got home later that night.

Sarah just stared at him for a few moments and then with an almost terrified look on her face responded, "Oh, Tommy; what have I gotten myself into?"

CHAPTER `4

The Day After

"WHAT'S THE SCORE again?"

"30 love"

"Oh, okay, how is it that we always forget!" laughed Katherine as she ran back to await the next serve.

"I never forget!" announced Brittany.

The ball flew past Katherine like a rocket, followed quickly by a second.

"Geez, take it easy on me!"

"I play to win, Katherine. If I take it easy on you, it's not going to help my game at all. That makes it 40 love."

"Hey, by the way, thanks for coming with me last night. That was fun, wasn't it?" said Katherine as she approached the net.

"Hmm, let's just say it was different," answered Brittany.

"Ha ha, yeah, I know it wasn't anything like what you're used to, but that reminds me, why on earth did you volunteer to be one of the members of their club?"

"Well obviously it's not because I'm interested in free labor from a bunch of unqualified women!"

Katherine's face flushed, and she fired back, "OBBBviously!"

"Well you know my ongoing challenge with David and his study . . . and there was something she said about a home telling a story that intrigued me."

"Yes, but she's expecting all of the members to roll up their sleeves and help each other. I can't see you doing that kind of manual labor, or any, for that matter," laughed Katherine.

"Oh, I have no intention of doing it!"

"Well then what are you going to do?"

"I'll just show up and bide time until it's my turn. Hopefully that comes fast. Besides, Katherine, I'm quite sure these women don't know the first thing about quality."

"What do you mean by quality?" asked Katherine.

"Well let's face it, you've seen my house. It's filled with nothing but the best."

They should be grateful to just have me in their presence and if they all take notes, maybe they'll learn a thing or two. Ha ha, maybe that's my true calling, you know, to help all those less fortunates out there," laughed Brittany.

"Yeah, right, I can see that," muttered Katherine under her breath.

* * *

The clock on the nightstand read 7:35. Tabatha jumped out of her bed and sprinted to the shower as if the starting gun had just gone off at one of her many previous competitions. Although the anxious feeling inside her stomach was unlike any sensation she had ever experienced before an upcoming race. But today would definitely prove to be a marathon day; it would be one of a quite different nature.

While Tabatha was counting on her stamina to get her physically through the next several hours, she had trepidations from an emotional point of view as to whether or not she would be able to make it across the finish line.

Mindlessly, Tabatha toweled off and began getting dressed. She blew her shoulder-length auburn hair dry and almost robotically applied her foundation, blush and mascara.

She then slipped into her favorite black pumps and ran back to her bathroom mirror for one more look.

"Oh my gosh, what am I doing? This is all wrong!"

Tabatha then reached her right arm behind her neck grabbing hold of the dress zipper and began tugging it all the way down until the outfit opened and she was able to free herself. It then fell resting on the bathroom floor.

"This is really going to put me behind schedule now, but I can't wear a black dress, not today!"

Tabatha quickly went back to her closet and began riffling through her hangers, stopping at a pretty peach pantsuit.

"Hmm, I think this is much better," she concluded.

Within the next 4 minutes, Tabatha was redressed and fleeing out her garage door. Now buckled into her Firebird, she backed out of her driveway and began the 20-minute trek to All Saint's Church.

"Welcome everyone. I'm Pastor Dave. I'm going to ask you to please take a seat. We will be starting momentarily. I'm sorry for the delay; but today's key speaker had something unavoidable pop up at the last moment. But the good news is she's here now, so please join me in welcoming Tabatha Benson."

The auditorium was filled with the sound of clapping hands. Tabatha nervously waited for the applause to slow down before speaking.

"Thank you, everyone. I'm honored to be here with you today." Taking a deep breath, she began.

"I'm nobody special. I don't have a television sitcom nor an album topping any charts. I'm not married to a billionaire and don't own a castle in France. I'm just Tabatha, who, like all of you, has lost a child. My husband Eric and I had only one; her name was Madeline. She was the light of our world. Not only was she beautiful, but she was kind, loving, caring and very talented."

Tabatha paused for a moment and then continued. "She was a concert violinist and had actually landed a seat with the New York Philharmonic. We were so very proud of her. Madeline started playing the violin when she was just four years old. It was all she thought of until she met Nick. My son-in-law was also very loving, kind and caring. He was an ER doctor at Lennox Hill hospital in New York. Nick too was an only child, but both his parents were deceased.

"Seven years ago, my baby gave birth to twin boys. Their names are Taylor and Ryan. When they were six months old Madeline and Nick entrusted them to us and went away on a much-needed vacation. They had only been in Mexico for two days when they were struck by a drunk driver in a head-on collision. That man not only robbed Eric and me of our beautiful daughter and amazing son-in-law, but he left our two grandbabies without ever knowing their mommy and daddy," Tabatha said passionately while trying to suppress her emotions.

"And the thing that makes this even more devastating is that that man walked away with not even a scratch!" Tabatha exclaimed through tears.

The room went silent, and as Tabatha looked around, she could see the majority of attendees wiping their eyes or reaching for tissues. That gave her the strength she needed to continue.

"But I'm not here today to say my loss is any more horrendous than any of yours. The bottom line is it's a terrible pain each of us share no matter what the circumstance. The important question now is how do we move on? I don't know about all of you, but the last thing I wanted to do was move on, because that meant I had to let go, and I wasn't ready to let go!

"For a long time, I was so angry at God. I couldn't understand why He let this happen. Why did He take my baby? Then one day I woke up and realized I had a new purpose in life. I now had two little boys who needed me desperately and a loving husband who was going through his own pain who also needed me. It was time for me to put on my big-girl pants and stop thinking about just myself and my pain.

"I still don't know exactly what God's plan is for me or for any of you, for that matter. But, I do know He has a purpose for each of us, and it's not just to hold onto the past.

Thank you for listening to my story, and I pray that in some small way it helps you to let go of the past and live on. Thank you again."

* * *

"Hey, Tricia, I'm home. Where are you?" Paul said as he closed the front door.

"I'm upstairs in the spare room," Tricia shouted back.

Paul ran up the stairs and down the hall stopping just outside the bedroom door. Resting his arm on the molding, he began his one-sided conversation, "What are you doing in here, Trish? Oh, and have you washed my coaching shirt? I didn't see it in my drawer. I need that today because we have a game. My brother Kenny called me today—Savannah wants to know if you have work on the fifteenth."

"Why does she want to know if I have work?"

"Oh, she wants to know if you can babysit."

"What a surprise! That's all she ever wants. Good old Aunt Tricia, she doesn't have a life so she can be our babysitter. She's such a jerk. I can't stand her!"

"Don't you think you're being hard on her? She's not that bad. I mean, sure you don't have that much in common, but I think she really likes you. Besides if she didn't, she wouldn't ask you to watch the kids."

"Are you kidding me? That was a stupid thing to say! I'm free labor; that's all she's interested in! And, yeah, you're right; we don't have anything in common. She spends her days going out to lunch with Buffy and Barbie while I work. She has two picture-perfect kids that she dresses up like a prince and princess, and I have this ugly doll she left here on purpose to remind me of how wonderful her life is."

"What do you mean she left the doll here on purpose?" fired back Paul.

"She left the doll to remind me that I don't have any kids!"

"Trish, I think you're going a little too far on that one. She wouldn't be that hurtful. I'm sure she just forgot it."

"Oh; you don't think so? Two weeks ago she called me up and told me how filled her heart was and just felt that she needed to share. She then went on the attack and told me that she didn't know what my problem was, but regardless she viewed herself as the family's savior. For she and she alone has been able to provide your parents with not one but two grandchildren. She said it made her heart so happy to see what joy little Wyatt and little Aubrey bring to them. So don't tell me I've gone too far!"

"Oh, I didn't know. Sorry Trish. By the way, how was your time out last night at the new neighbor's house? Did you have fun?" Paul asked desperate to change the conversation.

"It was alright I guess. A bunch of us are joining a club that she's starting."

"Cool, what kind of club?"

"A decorating club."

"Wow, I'm surprised!"

"Why are you so surprised?" Tricia demanded.

"Well, I mean it just seems more of a girlie thing, and I guess I never viewed you quite like that. It's not as if you've taken a big interest in decorating our house. I mean look at this room for example; you've never done anything with it. It just sits empty."

"Just because I have six older brothers doesn't mean I'm not a girl!" shouted Tricia. I am a girl! What do you want out of me, Paul? I work all the time. I'm not like you, who gets out every day at five and then gets to go play on the field with a bunch of kids. I have very little time to do anything, not to mention anything I want to do for myself!"

*　*　*

"Hello, Mrs. Patel, please follow me." Reshma, holding Lilly in her arms, got up from the chair and followed the young girl down the hall to examining room 1.

"The doctor will be right in," she said, closing the door behind her.

Moments later the door reopened and in walked Dr. Stephen Allen a.k.a. Dr. Dreamboat to most of Crofton's female population.

"Mornin', how's it going, Reshma?"

"Oh, hello, Dr. Steve. I'm fine, thank you. How are you?"

"Reshma, how many times do I have to tell you to just call me Steve? We're neighbors for Pete's sake."

"Okay D . . . I mean Steve. I will try."

"So this is a big day for Lilly, her very first dental checkup. Are you excited, Lilly? Okay let's count those teethies, kiddo," said Steve while gently opening Lilly's mouth. "So I hear you and my Jackie are taking on the design world with a couple of the other neighbors."

"Oh yes. I'm not sure how well I will do though. I have never done anything like this before."

"Well, Jackie told me that nobody needs experience and that the new neighbor was going to teach everyone. I think that's great! Jackie's really looking forward to it, and she said she could use something to occupy her time. It's kind of quiet now that the kids are all out of the house. Maybe you girls will make me a man cave. I'd be good with that!" joked Steve.

"You're doing good, Lilly, only a few more minutes, baby girl."

"How about you, Reshma, do you have a redo room in mind?"

"I think I will need to study more on what American homes should look like for I'm not sure, but I think mine still needs the 'do' part before the redo," Reshma said with all sincerity.

"Ha ha ha, that's funny, Reshma!" Steve said, finishing up with the checkup. "Okay, ladies, we'll have you back again in six months. Bye for now. Cheerio!"

CHAPTER 5

House Rules

HONK. HONK. HONK. Honk, the horn sounded for the fourth time.

"Ugh, what am I doing? That's so annoying," Sarah thought to herself as she consciously removed her finger from the button of her car's remote. "Besides, this is supposed to be fun. I don't know why I'm so nervous."

Sarah opened the door to the Dunkin Donuts and walked over to the counter. "Hi, Sarah, do you want your regular?" asked the store manager as she prepared to pour the hazelnut coffee into the extra-large Styrofoam cup.

"Yes, please, Natasha, and I'll also have an egg-and-cheese croissant today," she answered.

Happy to see that the place was empty, Sarah began to move several of the tables and chairs around creating one big table with seven chairs.

"Hi, Sarah, am I the first one here?"

Glancing over her shoulder, Sarah saw a tall, heavyset woman in an unmistakable Lilly Pulitzer dress with pink matching shoes. "Oh, hi, Maggie. Yes, you're first. How was your weekend?"

"It was okay. Mark had to work, and Daniella slept over at a girlfriend's house, so I went out with one of my friends on Friday night to California Kitchen. Saturday I got my hair done and simply stayed home, put on my pjs, made some popcorn, and watched a movie marathon. How about you?" Maggie asked as she flipped her hair from one side to the other.

"Oh, it was pretty good. You know, birthday parties, sleepovers, kids' sports, food shopping, laundry, the dog had to go to the vet, and I picked up the dry cleaning. Maggie, feel free to jump in and stop me anytime now," Sarah said with a smile.

"You sure are a busy woman, and I think it's wonderful how you've agreed to—"

"Hi, guys," said Tabatha, interrupting Maggie midsentence.

"Hi, Tabatha," responded the women. "We were just talking about the weekend. How was yours?" asked Sarah.

"Well my sister Heather is here visiting all month, so she told Eric and me to make the most of it and suggested we go away for the weekend." Pausing for a second, Tabatha laughed and then continued, "Trust, me neither of us needed much encouragement! Anyway, we had a really nice weekend. We stayed in Berlin and spent the day antiquing on Saturday, and then we stopped off at the factory outlets Sunday on our way back home."

"Where's Berlin? Did you fly to Germany for the weekend?" teased Sarah.

"No, you're funny. It's actually a great place to go though if you like antiquing. It's out on the Eastern Shore." Tabatha smiled.

"Did you find anything good at the outlets?" asked Maggie.

"Yeah, as a matter of fact, I got this whole outfit there," Tabatha replied, placing her hand on her hip and twirling around.

"Well it's beautiful and you look like a runway model for Ralph Lauren," said Sarah.

"Ah, you're sweet, thank you," said Tabatha.

Once again, the door opened. This time it was Brittany and Jackie followed closely by Reshma. Sarah also saw Tricia pulling into the parking lot and watched with curiosity as Tricia parked her car and then ran around to the other side as if she was inspecting it. Next she threw her arms into the air, looked up in what appeared to be a disapproving manner and stormed in to join them.

"Good morning, Tricia," Maggie said cheerily as Tricia approached the line and stood behind her.

"What's so good about it?"

"Why? What's wrong?" Maggie inquired.

"I'll tell you what's wrong—the stupid truck driver who just cut me off causing me to run up the curb and take a chunk out of my right tire and dent my hubcap is what's wrong; I hate my life," she muttered to herself while pulling her long blonde hair into a tight ponytail.

Over the next ten minutes, one by one, each of the women had gotten their order and were seated; then Sarah began, "Good morning, guys, and thanks for coming here today. I know it's been a while since the party, and you were probably wondering if we were ever going to get started! I'm sorry it's taken so long, but I wanted to have a chance to think about how this would all work and make sure I was ready."

"That's okay, Sarah, we know where you live!" giggled Maggie.

"Yeah, and now we also know you're real!" chimed in Tricia.

"Ha ha, thanks, guys!"

Sarah picked up a stack of cards and began passing one to each of the women. "Okay, now don't laugh, but I have a membership card for all of you."

"A membership card? What are we in kindergarten again, Sarah? Is our name printed on it?" asked Tricia as she took hold of hers and started to inspect it.

"Well, let me put it this way, it's true what they say: membership does have its rewards, and if you want any of them, you'll need this card." Sarah then picked up the next pile of papers and once again passed one to each member. "Now this is a list of all the companies in our area that believe in the philosophy of the Decorating Club and want to support us by offering a discount on their products, services or both!" said Sarah excitedly.

"Wow, that's really cool," said Reshma.

"Yes, I think so too. Most of them told me how happy they were to sponsor our efforts of neighbors helping neighbors and that's why this sheet is labeled 'Decorating Club Friends and Supporters.'

"Now on to business. The next thing we need to do is set up working committees for each of the various activities we'll be working on. For instance, to start with we'll need a painting committee, a sewing committee and an accessory committee as well as flooring and lighting committees. Obviously, with only seven of us, I'm going to ask everyone to serve on at least one committee, and we'll need to appoint a leader of each. That person will be responsible for setting the schedule, arranging field trips and so on, any questions?"

"Oh, Sarah, I have a question."

"Sure, Maggie, go ahead."

"Well I'm certainly not the best painter in the world, but I can roll on paint. So do you mean that I need to know how to do all those fancy paint techniques to be on the committee, 'cause honestly I don't know how to do any of them, only regular painting?"

"Great question, Maggie! No, you don't have to know any faux paint techniques. We're all going to learn from one another, and the things we don't know we'll be looking to seasoned experts to teach us—and that applies not only for the painting committee but every other one as well. In fact, I suspect there'll be times when we simply opt to move into the general contractor or 'GC' role and oversee others instead of performing the work ourselves. Anyway, that's a decision each of you can make as we move forward.

"Now just a few more things," Sarah continued. "While each homeowner will be solely responsible for the costs of their project, we all share the responsibility for helping each other out by bringing and using our own tools, like ladders, sewing machines, paint brushes, etc."

"Oh, that's clever. I mean why go out and spend the money on tools if we all already have our own. I'm sure most of us own at least one paintbrush and probably a couple of tape measures. That is, if you guys are anything like me. Ha ha, I can never find that darn thing when I need it, and so I always end up buying another one," admitted Tabatha.

"Agreed," said Sarah. "Oh, before I forget," she continued, "the project owner is also responsible for 'fuel' costs. You know things to keep us all going, like coffee and sugary goodies.

"And lastly, once a project is finished, I was thinking it might be fun for us to celebrate in that member's home with a cocktail party—and if the guys promise to get off the couch and dress up a little maybe we'll invite them too," Sarah teased.

"I think that's a wonderful idea. We'll have to make sure we take before, during and after photos so we can dazzle them with our handiwork," volunteered Tabatha.

"Great idea. Okay that's it, and now, just to make it official, I ask everyone to raise their right hand and repeat after me—I, (say your name), having been admitted as a new member of the Decorating Club, do so hereby solemnly swear, upon my honor, to help, encourage and support my fellow members to the best of my ability. I further promise to step out of my own comfort zone and be willing to try, learn from my fellow members and share my own gifts and talents with them. All these I pledge and promise to do and observe without reservation, so help me God."

"This is too funny." Tabatha giggled. "I mean it's so formal, like we all now belong to some secret society."

"I agree, complete with our own code of ethics," laughed Jackie.

"Trust me, I'll definitely be keeping it a secret," said Brittany.

"Well I think it's cute, Sarah," said Maggie.

"Yes, I'm very excited!" exclaimed Reshma. "I've never heard of anything like this back in my country."

"Yeah, and I guarantee you won't hear about it here either. I feel like a nerd," muttered Tricia.

"Well, regardless, I just wanted you guys to take this seriously. I mean in my experience people will say one thing but do another. And if we're going to make this club a success, we all need to be on the same page, don't you agree?"

Just then, Natasha came from behind the counter and walked over to the group.

"Hey, Sarah, I overheard you talking, and I think the club sounds like a terrific idea. Maybe that's something I could join in on in the future. But anyway, right now I'd also like to become one of your supporters, if you're interested, and offer you guys a discount on every pound of coffee you purchase from us."

"Thanks, Natasha, that's awesome," said Sarah.

"Um, excuse me," interrupted Maggie, "but I was wondering, will you also be giving us a discount on the donuts too?" she questioned as she crossed her fingers and smiled.

CHAPTER 6

Your Style or Mine

ONCE THE GIGGLES finally settled down from Maggie's donut question, Sarah continued, "One of the most important things as it relates to designing or redesigning is to know your sense of style.

The 'feeling' that best represents you and what you want your home's interior to reflect," began Sarah.

"Um, Sarah, I don't think I have a sense of style," admitted Reshma.

"I think mine is 'over-cluttered.' Is that a style, Sarah?" joked Jackie.

"Yeah, I agree, I don't think I have a style either," volunteered Tabatha.

"Well it may surprise you to know that today there are lots of inspired styles including Art Deco, Arts and Crafts, Asian, coastal, contemporary, country, English country, French, French country, Mediterranean, transitional and the list goes on and on. Even eclectic is considered a style. Personally, that happens to be my favorite. I'm not quite sure if I like it best because it's more of a catch-all flair that borrows from several other design styles and evokes a sense of imagination and surprise, or if it's just because I like saying the word eclectic." Sarah laughed.

"Anyway, I have a folder here for each of you. Inside you will find a tab labeled 'Styles.' That's where you'll find a description for most of today's popular designs. This will be part of your homework."

"Homework!" interrupted Brittany.

"Yes, you heard me right," Sarah continued as she began passing out orange loose-leaf folders stamped with the words "My Redesign Plan" on the cover and personalized with each recipient's name printed below. "Actually I have lots of homework for you. In order for us to help each other, we need to understand better who you are. What things you like, what things you don't like, what your favorite colors are, where you like to go on vacation, the books you read, the music you listen to, and most importantly, your gifts and your talents. All of those questions you'll find under 'Who Am I?'" Sarah said as she handed out the last manual.

"Well my section is going to be filled with blank pages because I don't have any gifts or talents," barked Tricia.

"Yes you do, Tricia. Every one of us has gifts and talents. In fact, you might end up better understanding more about yourself in the process of simply exploring what they are, and then you can begin sharing them with us," countered Sarah. "Also, remember that you just pledged to all of us that you would." Sarah winked.

"In fact, I've learned that it's sometimes helpful to ask those who know us best for their insights. They often can see in us what we can't see in ourselves. In fact, a few weeks ago we unexpectedly had an experience that proves the point. It happened when Katie, our youngest, was complaining at dinner that she wasn't as good as the rest of the players on her soccer team. It seems that some of her teammates were saying mean things to her about being clumsy and slow and not knowing how to play. After several rounds of tearful outbreaks, Katie said, 'I'm not good at anything, am I?'

"Then before we could even comment, her siblings jumped in to tell her all the things she was really good at, and we were quite impressed by their keen insights about her abilities," admitted Sarah.

"Ah, that's so sweet and loving of them," said Tabatha.

"Yeah, Tommy and I were a little shocked. They're good kids but can still be mean to each other at times."

"Oh brother," said Tricia as she rolled her eyes. "That might be good for you and your little darlings, but I'm not good at anything, and if you ask everyone I know, they're going to still tell you the same thing."

"Just shut up, Tricia. We get it already. Boo-hoo, you don't have any talents. Let's keep this moving along. I have workers at my house and need to get back," Brittany said as she glanced at her watch.

CHAPTER 7

Who Am I?

THE ROOM WENT QUIET for a moment or two and then finally Tabatha broke the silence, "So, Sarah, whose house are we going to work on first?"

"Gee, I'm not sure, but I thought before we decided on that maybe we could spend a little more time getting to know each other better. I realize I'm the newbie of the community, but I bet there's a lot more to each of you than anyone knows. So I was thinking it might be fun if you all write down something about yourselves that you're sure no one else here knows. Then I'll collect the papers and read them out loud one by one, while we try to figure out who authored each statement," said Sarah.

"Oh, you mean like that old TV game show 'What's My Line?'" asked Jackie.

"Yes, that's exactly right," said Sarah.

***

A short while later, Sarah reached into her empty Dunkin Donuts cup, pulled out the first paper, and read aloud "I've met the queen. Who am I?" she said in a terrible British accent.

The room went quiet, then Jackie spoke, "I think it's Brittany."

"Yes. How did you know it was me?" she asked.

"I'm not certain, but somehow it just seems to fit," said Jackie.

"Well, I'm not sure what that's supposed to mean, but, yes, I was actually a congressional intern at the time. It was in May of 1991, and the queen of England came to address a joint meeting of Congress," Brittany said matter-of-factly.

"Wow, did you curtsy for her?" asked Tabatha.

"No, I did not. I certainly wasn't going to look like a prat," declared Brittany.

"What's a prat?" questioned Maggie.

"Prat is a British term for a stupid, incompetent or foolish idiot. You're not supposed to curtsy when you meet the queen, and actually, her formal title is 'Your Majesty' and that's how you should address her when you meet her for the first time. After that, you call her 'ma'am.' You have to follow proper etiquette when and I should say if you're ever lucky enough to meet the queen," said Brittany with an air of arrogance.

Just then, Tricia stood abruptly pushing back her chair while bending down into a very proper curtsy. "Hey, guys, look at me. I'm a prat! I'm a prat!"

Brittany just shook her head and said, "Yes, you clearly are!"

"Hmmm, okay, that was very interesting," said Sarah. "Now let's continue. 'I was my high school homecoming queen. Who am I?'"

"I think it's Tabatha," said Brittany.

"Nope, I think it's Sarah," said Tabatha.

"Thank you, but, no, it's definitely not me. Any other guesses?" asked Sarah. "Nobody? Okay then, will the real homecoming queen please reveal her identity?"

"I know it's hard to believe looking at me now, but it was actually me, about a hundred pounds ago," said Maggie as she tugged at her dress.

"Well I can see that. You have a beautiful face, Maggie," offered Tabatha.

"Yes, and I think you look great, Maggie," said Reshma.

"Thank you, that's very kind, but I could use to lose some weight. In fact, I'm thinking of starting a new diet next week. I want to lose at least twenty pounds before I have to go with Mark to one of his work events that's coming up soon. Hey, have any of you heard of the radish diet? You're supposed to eat a cup of radishes before every meal and then they say the weight just melts off."

"Cool," Sarah said, swiftly reaching into the cup and pulling out the next paper. "'I was on my high school debate team. Who am I?'"

"Oh, I know, I know," said Maggie excitedly waving her hand in the air. "It's got to be Tricia."

"Well we could debate it, but actually it was me," said Reshma quietly.

"Ha ha," said Tricia as she scowled at Maggie.

"Okay, moving right along. Now this one really cracks me up - 'I once stopped a wedding and married the groom. Who am I?'" asked Sarah.

"Wait, what?" asked Brittany.

"I don't understand. How can one do that?" asked Reshma.

"I'll tell you how one can do that: by being good at fishing," barked Tricia.

"So you fished for your husband?" Tabatha giggled.

"Very funny. No. I was in Key West on some captain's boat fishing with my brothers when I hooked a humongous tarpon. It was fighting me for more than two hours! Every time I got the fish close to the boat, it would take off again. The captain even strapped a belt on me to keep me inside the boat, and my brothers took turns dousing water on me. My hair was all flat, my clothes were wet and I had mascara dripping down my face—I was quite the sight based on the pictures.

"After I finally managed to bring the fish to the boat and the captain tagged it as a legitimate catch, I heard tons of screaming and yelling. I knew a lot of it was for me because I could hear people shouting 'congratulations' over and over again. But later after we docked, I found out that the screaming part was coming from a large yacht nearby," said Tricia.

"Why?" asked Sarah.

"Well apparently a couple were on the yacht getting married at the time, but when the whole wedding party spotted me fighting with my seven-foot, two-inch monster, they decided to pause the ceremony so they could watch."

"What? Seven feet, two inches? That's huge! Are you sure, Tricia?" asked Jackie.

"Yes, I'm sure. I have a paper that says it!" fired back Tricia.

"Wow, that had to be one big fish," said Tabatha as she raised her hands up over her head.

"I'm five eleven, so it would have to be at least this big."

Tricia continued, "Well unfortunately, or rather, fortunately for me, the bride got really mad. Then when the groom told her not to take life so seriously, it made her even madder, and she canceled the wedding! Later the former groom came to congratulate me. Then my brothers asked him to join all of us for a beer, and well, what can I say?" Tricia said.

"Oh my gosh, that is too funny," screamed Brittany.

As the laughter started to settle down, Sarah once again reached into the cup and pulled out the next paper. "Okay, this one reads: 'I was once a cheerleader for the Dallas Cowboys. Who am I?'"

"Oh, wow, that's really cool," said Jackie.

"Well? Any guesses?" inquired Sarah. "I think it's Jackie," volunteered Tricia without skipping a beat.

"Me, why do you think it's me? Is it the way I shake my pom-poms?" she laughingly asked while swinging her hips from side to side.

"Nope, I think it's you because you made a comment after it was read, and I think you're trying to throw us all off track!" answered Tricia.

"Well I'm sorry to disappoint you, Tricia, but give me a C, give me an O, give me a W, give me a B, give me an O, give me a Y and give me an S, and what's that spell? The mighty, mighty Cowboys!" chanted Tabatha.

"Well I can see that, Tabatha, you always seem so happy and positive. I bet you made a great cheerleader," said Sarah.

"Thanks, Sarah, although the truth is I've had my share of uncheerable moments," she replied with a wink.

Sarah pulled out the next piece of paper. "I almost made it to the Olympics as a figure skater, but I broke my ankle two days before going. Who am I?"

"Hmm, does it say what year it was, Sarah?" asked Tricia.

"No, Tricia, it doesn't," answered Sarah.

"Why do you want to know the year?" demanded Jackie.

"Because I thought it might give insight into the person's age," answered Tricia.

"Well it was 1980, and I guess it's obvious now that the klutz was me!" remarked Jackie.

"That's terrible, you must have been so disappointed," added Reshma.

"Yes, I was. I spent a great deal of my childhood on skates always working hopefully toward one day making it to the Olympics. I'm only glad it wasn't held somewhere like China or Russia, or I would have been really disappointed," said Jackie.

"Where was it held?" Brittany asked.

"Oh, it was held at Lake Placid. Don't get me wrong, that's still very cool, but I used to go there for family vacations all the time with my parents, so it wasn't like it was somewhere new or exotic to me," she shared.

"Do you still skate?" asked Brittany.

"No, I gave it up years ago when I started to have my family. Raising four kids with all their activities left very little if any time for me to even think about skating again. Although now with them gone I have all the time in the world," she said with a smirk.

Some would classify Jackie and Steve as almost "empty nesters," a title Jackie wasn't very happy with. She said she preferred to look at themselves "more like part-time landlords since our children are always coming and going. Besides, I have a hard time viewing my four kids as birds. While they may twitter and tweet, it's hardly the kind that would bring music to your ears, and the concept of eating like a bird is totally foreign in our family. In fact, every time all of them are home together, our food costs go through the roof!"

The girls laughed at Jackie's comments, but each could sense there was pain behind her witty sarcasm. Staring blankly off into space, Jackie continued, "And while they like to think they can soar with the eagles, the funny thing is almost all of them suffer from motion sickness. Yeah they sure drive me nuts, but I have to admit, the house is noticeably barren when they're not around. I don't know, but somehow it seems that when they're young we trick our minds into thinking these days will never come or at least it's not something we need to worry about just then because it's still a lifetime away. But, boy, once they hit middle school, the time just rolls on by."

The room went quiet as they watched Jackie wipe a tear that had rolled down her face leaving a black streak in its trail.

"Well," said Sarah as she reflected on Jackie's vivid examples, "that may be true, but I'd like to point out that there's a lot of empty nests around my house and I've yet to see a mother bird just sitting there waiting for her chicks to return. Hey, Jackie, I have an idea: why don't we make your home our first project. Does that sound okay to you?"

"Oh, wow, that'd be great—I mean if that's okay with the rest of the members," she questioned. "And I hate to sound greedy, but if it's not too much to ask, I actually have two rooms that really aren't being used; it's the bedrooms that my boys and girls shared. I have been thinking maybe we could do something with each, but I don't have a clue yet as to what."

"Alright, well let's make next Monday the official kick-off date, then, for the Decorating Club's first project. We'll all plan to meet at your house, Jackie, right after the school bus leaves. Does that sound good everyone?"

"Okay, that's perfect."

"Yup."

"Yes."

"I'm in."

"Sounds good."

"Um, okay, Sarah, I'll arrange my schedule and will be there, but aren't you forgetting something? You haven't read your paper yet," said Brittany.

"Oh, you're right," laughed Sarah as she reached into the cup taking out the last folded piece of paper.

"'I had a provocative role on TV in a men's shaving commercial. Who am I?'"

"Oh my gosh!"

"I can't believe that!"

"What do you mean by provocative?"

"Come on, what do you think it means? We're all adults here! It means she probably showed some skin."

"Oh wow, Sarah, you definitely are filled with surprises!"

"Was Tommy okay with that?"

"Well, Tricia is right, I definitely did show some skin, and as far as Tommy being okay with it, he wasn't then, but he is now," said Sarah.

"Oh my gosh, Sarah, well that's good. I mean at least he's okay now with it," said Maggie.

"Yes, but let me explain, it wasn't that Tommy was not okay with it from the start; it was just that he didn't know about it then."

"Oh, Sarah, that's a shame. It's never good to keep secrets no matter how tough things are, honey," said Jackie.

"No, no, no! The reason Tommy didn't know about it is because it happened many, many years ago. You see it was a shaving commercial for Hidesman Shave! They showed a bunch of men clothed in skins with long beards, and at the end of the commercial they made reference to their faces now being as smooth as a baby's bum, and well, that's when they showed my derriere on the screen."

"HA ha ha, that is so funny!"

CHAPTER 8

Purpose

Project #1 - Jackie

THE FOLLOWING Monday came quickly, but not quick enough for Jackie, who suddenly felt a renewed sense of direction. It was a welcome feeling she realized had been lacking for quite some time. As the members filed into her house, they were greeted with the wonderful aroma of warm cinnamon buns and the smell of freshly brewed coffee.

"So where's the patient? Let's get a look-see," said Tricia.

"Oh, you mean the rooms? They're upstairs. Let's grab a cup of coffee first and then I'll take you up and show you," said Jackie.

Inside each room was pretty much what one would expect—a personal time capsule of each child. The boys' room was painted in shades of blue and brown with blue corduroy bedding. The dressers were cluttered with mementos and trophies, and the walls were covered with rock band posters and pictures of "angels" in skimpy bathing suits. The bedding in the girls' room had hues of pink and orange. Most of the walls were covered with cork and fabric boards crowded with pictures of girlfriends and boys, boys and more boys.

"Okay, now that we've seen the rooms, let's go back downstairs and work on your vision for them Jackie."

"Hey, wait a minute. Shouldn't we take some before pictures first?" questioned Maggie.

"Oh, you're right, Maggie. Good thought I almost forgot! Who wants to play photographer?" asked Sarah.

"I'll do it," volunteered Tricia as she pulled out her new phone.

"Thanks, Tricia, we'll meet you downstairs when you're done. Hey, Jackie, I hope you don't mind, but I'm going to help myself to some more coffee," said Sarah.

"Of course, Sarah, please help yourself, and if there's not enough I can make more."

"Okay, you may have too. Coffee is my middle name," laughed Sarah.

After refilling her cup, Sarah joined the rest of the girls and sat down at the kitchen table.

"Okay, Jackie let's see what you've got in your folder, and talk to us about what you would like to do with the rooms," said Sarah.

Jackie's appearance changed almost instantly. Her cheeks became flushed, her nostrils flared and her mouth clenched tightly.

It seemed as if several minutes had lapsed, but then finally Jackie spoke, "Well, to be honest with you, Sarah, I don't have any answers to the 'Who Am I?' section because frankly, I no longer know who I am."

Jackie suddenly raised her hands holding her fingers in a steeple-like position and pressed them against her lips as she continued, "It was a lot easier when the kids were young. Back then, I had several titles: I was Cookie Mom, Teacher's Aide, Scout Leader, Dr. Mom and so on. But now," she paused for a moment and then continued, "I'm just plain old Jackie who unfortunately spends most of her time feeling sad, lonely and quite frankly struggling to find a purpose," she lamented.

"Wow that's crazy!" thought Sarah. "I don't know what to say to make her feel better because it's almost as if we share the same problem, only from two completely different viewpoints. Jackie feels as if she's lost her purpose in life because it was centered around her children. In my case, I feel I've lost who and what I was before I became a mother and as a result now view my life solely as a caretaker.

"Ah, Jackie, you shouldn't feel that way. You do serve a purpose! And just because your kids are older doesn't mean you're done being a mom. They may not need you to wipe their noses, but they still need you in other ways," offered Maggie.

"Maggie's right. They may not need you in the same way as they did when they were younger, but they do still need you. For example, I think they need to see how you handle this stage of your life because one day they'll be sitting there with a choice to make of their own. You wouldn't want them to stop living just because their babies were all grown, would you?" asked Reshma.

"Yeah, and trust me, life can change in the blink of an eye. Then you may be called in to help them in ways you never thought imaginable. It's best not to be sitting there pining about the past because you never know what the future will bring," wrinkling her face as if she was in pain, she continued, "Ohh, I hope that didn't sound too preachy. I'm just passionate about living every moment as if it was your last," said Tabatha.

"No, Tabatha. I appreciate all of you kicking me in the butt. I have a lot to be grateful for. I've been in this slump for a while now, so I hope you'll all be patient with me as I try and dig myself out of it," said Jackie.

"Well I think this was a great first meeting, and honestly I too appreciate all the wisdom you guys offered today. Now, I have my sister coming for a visit this week, so would it be alright if we wait and meet again a week from Wednesday?" asked Sarah.

"Oh! Sarah I should have mentioned it earlier but the following week Steve and I are planning on going to Wisp Mountain. We have a little cabin up there and we go every year around this time." said Jackie.

"That sounds great, good for you guys. When will you be back?" asked Sarah.

"It's just for a week. Steve doesn't like being away from the office for too long," said Jackie.

"No problem, how about we make it the following week then?" offered Sarah.

"Ok, so are you saying two weeks from Wednesday then?" asked Reshma

"Yes, two weeks from Wednesday as long as that works for you guys," said Sarah.

The girls each nodded their heads yes except for Tricia who said, "I'm not sure what my shift will be yet but I'm sure I'll be able to get someone to switch if it becomes a conflict."

"Perfect! See you all in two weeks then," said Sarah.

Sarah chose to linger a few minutes longer and gently explained to Jackie how important it was for her to complete all the papers she had been provided. Especially the "Who Am I?" questionnaire since it would be the key to helping Jackie understand where she was.

"Would you like me to come back this evening and see if I can help you figure it out?" Sarah asked.

"Oh, that would be wonderful! I'd really appreciate it" Jackie replied. "Should I put on coffee?" she continued, knowing how much her new friend enjoyed it.

"No, that's okay; I'll introduce you to another beverage I enjoy. It's red, and requires no cream." Sarah giggled.

* * *

Later that evening, Sarah returned as promised, and with her came a bottle of red wine that she and Tommy discovered on vacation in Maui at a restaurant named Fleetwood's. They enjoyed the wine so much that they brought back a case. Earlier, Sarah had reflected on how much she liked tasting all of the wine's fruity notes and the peaceful and happy time Sarah spent while sharing it with Tommy on their trip. It was her hope that it might have a similar effect on Jackie.

As the bottle was uncorked, Sarah began peppering Jackie with questions about her life before kids and husband.

"Well you already know about my life as an almost Olympian," Jackie joked.

"Yes, that was really impressive, Jackie. I know it must have been sad for you and your parents, but you should be applauded for your strength and determination. You must have spent a huge amount of time practicing and perfecting your skill to be that good," acknowledged Sarah.

"Thanks, Sarah. Yes, as I look back at my childhood it seems that I was always either on the ice or at the base of my parents' sewing machines," explained Jackie.

"Did you say your parents' sewing machines? Your dad liked to sew?" questioned Sarah.

Jackie laughed so hard that she struggled to respond. "Oh, that did sound funny. No my father didn't sew doll clothes or anything like that. He was a tailor and made his money specializing in high-end custom suits. My mother, on the other hand, worked as a theatrical seamstress and sewed all kinds of colorful and creative costumes. If I wasn't skating, I often enjoyed spending my time on the floor of their workroom playing with bolt ends and discarded remnants of their beautiful fabric. I loved mixing and matching them while pretending I was some famous designer the world just discovered," Jackie said while waving her hand in front of her face and shifting her hips to the right.

"So, of course, it was a natural for me to later go to FIT, the Fashion Institute of Technology in New York City. That's where I earned my degree in fashion design with a minor in fashion management," Jackie proudly declared.

"Wow, so did you ever get to work behind the scenes at fashion week? My niece had the opportunity to intern with a designer, and she helped manage the models as they prepared for the runway!" said Sarah.

"No, it was a little different back then and a lot less glamorous, with a lot less opportunities. Some of my friends were runners for the fashion houses, though, meaning they moved clothing from one location to another." Jackie smiled. "But me, I took a job in a floral shop. I was lucky because FIT is right by the Flower District, which made it super convenient. Anyway, while working at the shop I learned how to make floral arrangements and set up for weddings."

"That must have been fun, but besides seeing a lot of lavish parties and beautiful gowns, what has that got to do with fashion?" Sarah asked.

Jackie tried to suppress her laugh, but sounding more like an old water faucet she continued, "Act-u-ally, it didn't have anything to do with fashion, I just needed the money! But really, it was a great experience and it gave me a valuable peek into designing wedding gowns as a possible career choice. Many of the gowns I saw just didn't match up with what I envisioned as a little girl—you know, magical! In fact, they all seemed pretty much the same with nothing special about them, and that always seemed to bother me. It was a long time ago, but sitting here with you Sarah, it all seems like just yesterday," Jackie reflected.

"Anyway, after graduation my parents sent me on a trip to England."

"Wow, that must have been cool; that's one place I've always wanted to go," said Sarah.

"Yeah it was beautiful and really a wonderful experience, but the best part was when I walked into a quaint little restaurant and found the man of my dreams inside." She smiled. "And the rest, as they say, is history."

"What! That's amazing, talk about an unforgettable souvenir!" Sarah laughed. "But seriously, did you ever do anything with your degree from school? I mean did you go on to work in the design field?" Sarah questioned.

"No!" Jackie sighed. "Unless you count all the clothes I've made for my daughters' Barbies and each one of my kid's Halloween costumes."

"That's a shame. Why not?" Sarah probed further.

"Well to be honest, I guess I was afraid and doubted that I was good enough. The last thing I wanted to do was disappoint my parents. Yet . . ." Jackie paused ". . . the funny thing is that while cleaning out their attic after they passed away, I found a file filled with tons of pattern pieces handmade by me.

"I never told this to anyone besides my parents but back then I was so enchanted with Cinderella that I wanted to make a dress just like hers. I remember spending every free minute I had working on it."

"That's impressive. How old were you?"

"Geez, Sarah, I'm not sure, but I was very young! As time went on, I made a whole collection of gown patterns. In my young mind I wanted to make sure I had several options for when my Prince Charming came along," Jackie said with a smile. "I never knew my parents kept all of them or how much they believed in me. It was only after going through the folder and reading all the notes did I come to realize it."

"What kind of notes?" asked Sarah.

"Oh, Sarah, I'll have to show you. Do you want to wait a minute and I'll run upstairs and get them?"

"Yes, of course, I would love to see them."

Moments later Jackie returned with an overstuffed file. As she prepared to put it down onto the dining room table, several notes and pattern pieces began slipping out onto the floor.

"Okay, I'm not going to bore you with all of them, but I'll read you a few," Jackie said as she picked up some of the ones that had fallen.

"To our bright and shining star we are so very proud of you."

"Jackie dear, there is nothing you can't do. Never let anyone tell you different."

"Good job! What do you think about making it all in satin?"

"Baby girl, you were born out of love and created for a reason, show the world who you are."

"This is fantastic, honey! Maybe consider using a crushed white velvet material with antique lace and satin trim."

"We will always love you! Love, Mommy and Daddy."

Sarah's eyes became glassy and filled with tears. She fought hard to hold them back, but as soon as she began to speak, a salty stray tear trickled down her face. Hearing all the encouraging words from Jackie's parents made her think about her own mom and how much she believed in Sarah.

"Oh, Jackie, how sweet. That made me cry," admitted Sarah. "There's nothing better than knowing how much our parents love and believe in us, is there?"

Sarah wiped away the tear and then continued, "Okay, I have to ask, do you still have a desire to design wedding gowns?"

"Yes," Jackie replied without hesitating. "I actually have filing cabinets filled with my designs, in hopes that one day my daughters may want me to make their dresses."

"So what are you waiting for?" Sarah encouraged.

"Well, um, none of them are engaged yet," Jackie softly stumbled.

"Oh, okay, I get that, but what about the rest of the world?" Sarah pressed. "Especially given what you just shared about it being a possible career choice. The way I see it, you grew up in an entrepreneurial family, you have natural-born talent that you continually improve upon on and you have a marketable gift that others will want. You also have two rooms available for you to turn into anything you desire, and I'm thinking one would make an amazing workroom!"

"Oh my gosh wow! That would be kind of cool. But I don't know, Sarah, it's been a long time. Besides, it's one thing to make your own daughters' wedding dresses, but to make them for complete strangers? I don't know; that's a different story."

"Yeah, but to be honest I don't think much has changed. I mean sure, there are a lot of gowns out there. Some are really wild and even borderline ridiculous, but it's like what you said; how many out there are magical? Who doesn't want that? After all, don't most of us want to star in our own fairy tale? I know I did! Promise me you'll at least give it some thought."

Jackie sat for a second in silence then nodded her head and said, "Okay, Sarah, I promise."

* * *

"Hello," said Sarah into the phone.

"Okay, Sarah, I'm here. Where are you? I thought you said you'd be here?"

"Hang on, Kara, I'm here. I'm not allowed to pull up until you're actually here."

"Well I'm actually here," joked Kara. "Don't you see me?"

"Is that you? Are you next to the wall? Kara tell me you're not wearing that ugly blue-and-red striped sweater I hate."

"Ha ha, I was wondering if you'd notice."

Sarah pulled around to the front of the BWI train station and stopped. "Come on, Kara, hop in."

Kara quickly climbed into the passenger side, leaned over, and gave Sarah a kiss. "Mwah. It's been a while, kid, but you look good."

"Thanks, Kara, you look pretty good yourself."

"Listen, the kids all have playdates today after school, so I was thinking maybe we'd go down to Annapolis and have lunch by the water. Does that sound good?"

"Yeah, that sounds great."

Approximately forty-five minutes later the two sisters were seated on the back deck of the Annapolis Waterfront Hotel, each sipping a Pusser's Rum Punch.

"This place is so cute; I love the Caribbean vibe. It makes me feel like I'm on vacation. Oops, I forgot—I am." Kara laughed.

"Yeah, it's one of my favorite places. I think you'd like the crab dip. Do you want to start with that?" asked Sarah.

"Well as they say, when in Rome . . . I mean I can't come to Maryland and not have the crab dip, can I?" teased Kara. "I went past your old house yesterday, Sarah. You won't believe how bad it looks."

"Why, what do you mean?" asked Sarah.

"Well for one thing I don't think they own a lawnmower 'cause the grass is so high! Plus, there's weeds everywhere and a bunch of junk in the driveway. I can only imagine what the inside looks like," Kara said.

"Well it's not my house anymore, so they can do what they want," said Sarah.

"Speaking of which, I can't wait to see what you've done with your new place!"

"Hey how's everything else going? Are you feeling a bit stronger about Mommy? Have you met many new friends? And, oh yeah, you have to tell me all about that Decorating Club you've started," said Kara.

"Stronger? I mean I guess so. But, it's still really hard for me to talk about her without crying. Oh, and I have this dream where she comes back to life but we all know it's only for a short time. It's really weird, Kara, and I keep having it over and over again," said Sarah.

"Yeah that is strange. Maybe she's trying to tell you something," said Kara.

"What would she be trying to tell me?"

"Geez, I don't know, Sarah. There was a time you seemed so unhappy. Maybe it's something to do with that," said Kara.

"It's not too easy to be happy when you find out your mom is dying and you're filled with fear from planes crashing into buildings," Sarah said defensively.

"I know, Sarah, but let's be honest; you weren't happy long before that. Don't you remember talking to me about whether or not there was more to life?"

"I remember; I mean I'm not perfect yet, but I am starting to see things differently now that I've been helping my friends decorate their homes," said Sarah.

"Do you mean because you're back to designing?" asked Kara.

"Well I mean maybe that's part of it. I do feel more valuable and less taken for granted than I did back home with some of my clients. But, I also think there's more to it. I feel like I'm helping them in other aspects. It's hard to explain, but in a lot of ways it seems like we all go through the same kinds of things, and I guess realizing that is somehow making me feel better."

"So what are you going to do when you're finished helping them? Are you going to restart your business?" asked Kara.

"I think I am, at least that's the plan right now. But, you know, Kara, maybe something else will come up. I have a feeling each of us serves more than one purpose. I may not know what it is at this exact moment, but I think as long as I keep moving forward and doing the things I'm led to do, it will eventually show up."

"Well said, baby sis. I'm proud of you. Remind me again who's older, you or me?" Kara said with a smile.

* * *

"Jackie if we don't leave now we might as well stay home!" shouted Steve from the driveway.

"Ok, I'll be right there I promise! I'm just going to run downstairs and grab some games for the kids," said Jackie as she hollered back from the garage.

A few minutes later Jackie returned with her arms filled with board games.

"Jack, where are you planning on putting those? There is no more room," insisted Steve.

Jackie carried her stash to the rear of the car and then utilizing every available space stuffed the games in before quickly slamming down the trunk lid.

"See, I told you they would fit," she said while buckling her seatbelt.

Without saying a word, Steve put the car in reverse and backed out of the driveway.

"Jack, what makes you think the kids are going to want to play games anyway? First of all, we're not a hundred percent sure any of them are even coming and if they do, I'm sure they'll be off running with their friends instead of sitting in the cabin playing games."

Jackie sat staring out the window for several moments then quietly said,

"I know but I brought them just in case."

"Listen, honey I don't mean to get you upset I just want to protect you.

Hey I don't think I told you but Theresa is quitting."

"Theresa your dental hygienist? She's been with you forever! Why is she quitting?" asked Jackie.

"She's going to start a cupcake business. She apparently loves making cupcakes and is pretty good at it. I'm happy for her but it was just such a surprise because she's always preaching to the kids about not eating too much sugar," chuckled Steve.

"Wow, that sure is a surprise, but you're in support of it? I mean do you think she could be successful at it even though she's never done anything like that before? After all, I'm sure it will be a lot of work just getting set up. Not to mention finding customers who are interested in her products. But, you think she can do it right? ...and you'd support her?"

"Sure! I believe she can make a go of it! Besides who doesn't like cupcakes?" laughed Steve.

A large smile formed on Jackie's face.

"Great!" she said. "I'm glad you feel that way because there is something I want to talk to you about."

CHAPTER 9

Plan On It

Where Am I Going?

THE DECORATING CLUB reassembled as planned, and as the team came into the house, the familiar aroma of baked goodies and the smell of freshly brewed coffee filled their nostrils.

But, this time, there was also something different in the air, not the aroma but the overall mood. It was Jackie; she seemed happy and full of life.

"Welcome, welcome. Come on in. How's everybody? Hey, Tricia, I love your jeans they look great on you. Oh, hi, Sarah, how was your time with your sister? Please make yourselves at home. It's great to see all of you again. Reshma, did you get a haircut? It looks beautiful.

"Don't be shy there's lots of pastries and homemade cinnamon buns. I hope you're all hungry. Wow, it's such a nice day today," said Jackie as one very long run-on sentence.

"What's with you, Jackie, did you have a hundred cups of coffee this morning?" asked Tricia.

"Ha ha, no, I guess I'm just happy to see all of you. Plus, I have some very exciting news to share!"

"That's wonderful. What is it, Jackie?" asked Sarah.

Jackie clenched her fist and then raised it up into the air. "Well, not only do I know what I want to do with each of the rooms, but now I also know what I want to do with my life!" she said cheerfully.

"Umm, wait a minute," said Tricia in a confused tone. "The last time I was here, you had no ideas for what you wanted to do with the rooms, not to mention your life, sooo, whaaa-happened?"

"Well, it all started after you guys left that first day. Sarah came back that night and we talked for a while," looking at Sarah she continued, "thank you again Sarah, you were so patient, kind and insightful and you have no idea what a difference your words made to me. Anyway, then I spent the rest of that week really going over the papers she gave me to fill out. I know none of us liked hearing that we would all have some homework to do for our projects – especially me! As that part I don't miss with my kids," she said half kiddingly. "But I really do think filling them out made all the difference. For they forced me to think about me, something I really haven't done in a long time. It was kind of like going through an old photo album. In my mind, I could see pictures of each stage of my life. As I glanced through all of the photos, I was able to zero in on some of my happiest moments.

"Then last week Steve and I drove up to the cabin and during our ride I had a chance to talk to him about my idea for the two rooms as well as a new plan for my life," said Jackie as she paused and gave way to a huge smile.

"Wait, this sounds really deep, please tell me you're not going to start a nursery school here for a bunch of bratty kids," said Tricia.

"No, Tricia I'm not going to start a nursery school. I did have other interests before becoming a mom you know," said Jackie.

"Oh yes I remember, you used to skate, right Jackie?" said Reshma.

"Yes Reshma, I did. I'm not sure I ever mentioned, but I also attended school at FIT for fashion design and have always been interested in designing wedding gowns."

"Oh wow, that's cool. My sister wanted to go there but she didn't get accepted," volunteered Tabatha.

"Well it was a great opportunity and I loved the school. Yet after I graduated, I never did anything else with my degree. Although I did constantly work on perfecting my gown designs. In fact, over the years I've sketched more designs than I can remember.

So I know this is a huge step but I've decided to go into business for myself, creating custom bridal dresses," declared Jackie.

"Oh my gosh, that is so cool," said Reshma.

"And so brave of you!" said Maggie.

"Okay, so you're not being very clear. Are you saying you're going to turn the two rooms into sweatshops?" inquired Brittany.

"No, I'm not saying that at all, Brittany! First of all, I'll be the only one making the gowns—just me and my machines."

"Then what are you going to do with the other room?" asked Brittany.

"I plan to convert the second room into my office. That's where I'll meet with my clients, the soon-to-be brides, to discuss their vision. But, I don't want it to be just like some ordinary office where I'd be sitting behind a desk. Instead, I want to model it after the restaurant where I met my husband, Steve.

"Sarah, the other night when you brought the bottle of wine over, you shared your desire and hope for me to feel as peaceful as you did when you drank it on your anniversary with Tommy, and that got me thinking."

Turning to the other women, Jackie continued, "You see, I met Steve in a little restaurant in England, and I remember it and the way I felt as if it was yesterday. It was a feeling of complete joy and happiness as I cherished each and every moment we spent together, while considering the possibility of someday living happily ever after with him.

"I thought it would be cool to recreate that same kind of atmosphere for my office. That way my clients and I can discuss gown designs over tea. I believe it will make for a much more relaxing experience," Jackie said.

"Wow that's wonderful, Jackie, and what a great example of capturing life in 3D," said Sarah.

"What do you mean by 3D Sarah?" asked Tabatha.

"Well, quite simply, it's an approach I have used that focuses on a creative combination of destination-based themes. By applying the 3D strategy—focusing on destination, decorating and dining—you can convert a flat and boring space into a vibrant, must-see destination brimming with atmosphere and charm.

"For instance, Jackie wants to recreate the little café where she met her husband, and we can definitely help her achieve the look. But, by going a step further and incorporating other senses, like sound, touch and taste, she'll be able to create a much more authentic environment. Then instead of flat or one-dimensional, the room will be filled with atmosphere and charm," explained Sarah.

"YES!"-shouted Jackie. "That's exactly what I want to do."

"Awesome! That's great, Jackie. Now we know where you are and where you want to go, so the next big thing we need to focus on is figuring out how you're going to get there," declared Sarah.

THE DECORATING CLUB

* * *

Decorating in 3D

Have you ever dreamed of living near the ocean? Perhaps a cozy little cottage in a quaint sea town or a magnificent mansion near the water's edge. Possibly, you were so smitten with last year's family vacation that you applied for a visa immediately upon your return home.

How about that adorable country inn in Vermont where you stayed and never wanted to leave? Or the spa in Georgia that not only recharged your body and mind but also enhanced your feelings of self-worth while surrounding you in luxury.

Trendy eateries, chic hotels, mountaintop resorts, cities in foreign countries, a wine cellar in Germany, a cruise to Alaska, behind home plate at Yankee Stadium; various snapshots of places you've been or perhaps of places you've always dreamed of going.

Now, can you close your eyes and visualize the way it looks, the way it sounds, the way it tastes and the way it smells? Better yet, can you describe how it makes you feel?

* * *

How am I going to get there?

"First thing we need to do is flesh out Jackie's vision. In other words, we need to put some flesh on the bones, so we can help her figure out how to get there."

"Oh yuck! Couldn't you use a better analogy?" complained Tabatha, a devoted vegan who was repulsed by the mere mention of the word meat.

"Geez, Tabatha, relax. If you want to talk about flesh and bones, you should see what I see in the operating room each day. In fact, just last week . . ."

"Okay, OKAY!" interrupted Sarah. "Let's not get off point. I'm sorry, Tabatha, I'll try not to use any more analogies or at least ones that may be perceived to be in bad taste.

"Now, Jackie, in order to help you to crystalize your vision for each of the rooms, you should start going through magazines and perhaps search the internet for inspiration. I also brought over a bunch of my design books for you to look at. There's a lot of great pictures of really well-designed rooms in them. I'm hopeful they'll provide you with some insight. Then after you've cut out magazine pictures or printed them off the web, just gather up all of your ideas and place them in separate folders. For instance, you might have folders for lighting, rugs, wall coverings, furniture, paint colors, fabrics, metals, florals, decorative accessories and so on—and here's a checklist that will help guide you."

"Okay, just to be clear, you want me to cut out pictures of things I like and put them in the corresponding files?" questioned Jackie.

"Yes, but not just what you like; it's also important for you to identify things you don't like and include them in your file together with notes that explain why. Now, while you're working on that, we'll start prepping by clearing out the two rooms. I have a box of black Hefty bags we can use to fill with trash or things designated for donations. This is actually a very important step in redesigning; I like to refer to it as 'weeding the garden.' Because by doing so, it allows space for the flowers to thrive and bloom. So unless there are any further questions, ladies, let's get started."

* * *

"How about this, Jackie, trash or donation?"

"And what about this?"

"Look at this. I'm thinking trash, am I right?"

It soon became clear that the questions were starting to make Jackie feel a bit overwhelmed and tense. But, it was only after Tricia's seemingly insensitive comment that Jackie reached her breaking point,

"OOOh this is definitely trash; it looks like a baby made it."

"Yes, that's right," snapped Jackie, "a baby did make it! My son made that in shop class when he was in sixth grade!"

"Well I think it's cute and you definitely need to hang on to those kind of things. Someday when you have a grandson or granddaughter you can show them what their daddy made you," said Tabatha.

"Exactly, I can't part with all these things!" said Jackie.

Taking a deep breath, Sarah started, "I know this might seem tough, Jackie, and it certainly can be emotional, but when you're redesigning, it's very important not to just hang onto things from the past. Remember we talked about this, even though those "things" may provide some level of security, they also tend to serve as a crutch preventing us from exploring possibilities that could lead us into other new and exciting directions.

"So why don't we just start another bag and we'll label it 'Kids.' Inside we can put all the things they've made, posters they've hung, trophies they've won, pictures of their friends and so on. Then later, you can go through it and decide what you might want to keep as well as what things you may want to toss."

"Or she can do what I did," volunteered Brittany.

"What that's, Brittany?" asked Sarah.

"I hired a carpenter to build me a separate room with lots of shelves. Now every time my kids make or give me something I have Consuela lock it in the 'no room room,'" said Brittany.

"The no room room? What the heck is that?" asked Tricia.

"Well as far as my children are concerned it's a special room I had created to house all their masterpieces and gifts to me and my husband. They believe it's because I don't want them being destroyed, and only Consuela and I have the keys. But it's really because there is so much clutter I don't want it messing up my house," said Brittany.

"W-h-a-t-t-t-t? Oh my gosh, you are so heartless. What kind of mother locks away their kids' gifts and art work?" asked Tricia.

Brittany stood and before heading for the door looked Tricia straight in the eyes and said, "Obviously you wouldn't understand." Then looking back over her shoulder she said, "Alright, Sarah, I have people waiting for me, so just call and let me know when we'll be doing this again."

"What a snob!" Tricia said as her lips went on to snarl as Brittany left.

CHAPTER 10

Sharing the Load

THE FOLLOWING DAYS and weeks brought a great deal of structure to the Decorating Club as they continued to work on Jackie's vision. Now that the rooms had been cleaned and stripped of all previous possessions, the girls were able to address the design elements that needed to be introduced within each room. In other words, they could better understand what, if anything would stay the same and what needed to change.

With the project plan Jackie completed for her new workshop and adjoining office as their guide, the women developed the desired look as well as the plan of attack.

* * *

The girls' room would be re-purposed to serve as Jackie's workroom. The oversized room was an obvious choice since it would provide plenty of space to work and could house all of Jackie's material and equipment. That the room received a great deal of natural lighting and offered an amazing view were simply added perks.

Design Element: Flooring

Jackie and Steve had recently replaced the worn-out orange shag rug with a new cream-colored low-pile carpeting. Since it wasn't very old and was still in perfect shape Jackie decided to keep it.

Design Element: Lighting

The next design element to be addressed was lighting. Although Jackie was thrilled with all the natural lighting, it wasn't adequate for night work or on cloudy days. After giving it some thought, everyone agreed that track lighting seemed to be the perfect solution and went on a field trip to Lowes where Jackie found the perfect fixture.

Design Element: Wallcovering

Jackie excitedly shared her file on wall covering ideas. "Now I know this might sound silly," she started, "but in creating the look and feel for my workroom, I believe it's important for me to keep my competition in mind."

"What's that supposed to mean?" demanded Tricia.

Jackie smiled and took a deep breath before answering. She was beginning to understand the need to anticipate comments and questions like this from Tricia.

It was just her way, and Jackie knew Tricia didn't mean anything by it.

"Well," she continued, "I used to love to visit Kleinfeld's Bridal, a world-class bridal salon located in Brooklyn. From the outside, it just looks like a regular three-window storefront, but once you step inside it's a whole other world, and to me it's simply magical!

"I thought if I could capture that type of feeling in my workshop it would remind me to always aim high. Besides, I intend to model myself after those I admire for their success and learn from their experience. But don't get me wrong, I don't have any delusions about taking on Kleinfeld's—at least not yet." Jackie winked.

"Wow, that's very cool. You already sound like a successful entrepreneur to me," said Reshma.

"Thanks, Reshma," said Jackie.

"You know I used to live right by Kleinfeld's–it was only for a few months, while Anil was in New York working on a special work project. In fact, I remember passing by their window almost every day," said Reshma.

"Oh, I'm jealous," said Jackie. "I would be there all the time if I lived that close. Did you ever go in?"

"No," replied Reshma.

"Well I bet you saw a lot of brides going in and out," stated Jackie.

"No," said Reshma.

"Didn't you even peek in the window?" asked Tabatha.

"No," said Reshma.

"Wow, you sure like the word no," teased Tabatha.

"I'm sorry; I guess it's just that I don't have a lot to say. My parents always told me and my sister that kids were to be seen and not heard," said Reshma.

"Ha ha, my parents told us the same thing," said Tricia.

"Oh, I thought that was something just parents in Bombay said." Reshma giggled.

"Are you kidding? I think all parents say that, but it was even more appropriate in my house growing up with all my big-mouth brothers," said Tricia.

"Well getting back to your walls, Jackie, I was wondering if you meant that you want to cover them in fabric?" asked Sarah.

"That would be cool, but honestly it would be way too expensive. I'm really not sure what I want to do. I just figured if I gave you some background it might help spark an idea or two. Did it work?" Jackie asked while crossing her fingers.

"Well, why don't you just take a big picture of Kleinfeld's building, put it in a frame and hang it on the wall of the workshop?" said Tricia in her characteristically sarcastic manner.

"I have an idea," said Sarah as she tried to ignore the last comment. "Since you're looking for an elegant feel, you might consider a faux paint technique. There are many beautiful and unique designs that you can create with paint. In fact, I'm thinking maybe something in a metallic or pearl finish could provide just the look you're searching for. How about I go through my collection of sample boards and pick out some for you to consider," offered Sarah.

"I love the idea, Sarah. Thank you. That would be great!" Jackie excitedly replied.

* * *

A few days later Sarah stopped by to show Jackie three sample boards. One was a white pearl finish achieved by using a large metal trowel. The second was a sponge painting application and the third was a linen weave technique.

"I love them all, but I think it would be amazing to have the walls look like real linen and certainly a lot less expensive. But who will we get to do that?" questioned Jackie.

"Everyone on the painting committee," answered Sarah.

"Hmmm, well now that we're by ourselves, that's something I wanted to revisit with you. I mean, what if it doesn't come out good?" Jackie questioned.

"Don't worry. First of all, it's only paint, and the great thing about paint is, you can always start over! In addition, think about all the money you'll be saving by having the members do it; faux finishes can be very expensive if you have to hire someone.

"Besides, everyone agreed to step out of their comfort zone, roll up their sleeves and try—you never know, maybe we'll discover a new Picasso in the process! But seriously, don't worry; I have a friend who is a professional specializing in faux finishes that I worked with back in New Jersey. He relocated to Annapolis a few years back, so I reached out to him, and he's agreed to host a sample board session in his studio. I plan to schedule a field trip for us to go next week. That way we will each have a great opportunity to learn and have plenty of time to practice.

"Plus, he's also available for hire, has agreed to be one of our Decorating Club Supporters and will even be offering a discount on his services. So really, you have nothing to worry about," Sarah said lightheartedly.

Sample Board Session

It was Wednesday at 10:00 a.m. sharp; when the girls on the painting committee all piled into the studio of Francois Chastain.

The space was perfect in size, neither too big nor too small. Yet the hundred or so brightly painted canvases definitely gave way to a crowded feeling. The area felt warm if not borderline hot due to the constant stream of natural lighting that brilliantly flowed in from the oversized windows.

The smell of turpentine was instantaneous and competed against all the other senses for attention. The only furniture was an antique wooden desk that sat in one corner of the room and a large overstuffed metal cabinet next to it with a puddle of art supplies that had fallen out onto the floor in front of it.

A constant drip coming from the paint-splattered sink was barely detectable due to the camouflage of coffee cans filled with paintbrushes. A huge demonstration board took up the anterior of the room with three large folding tables positioned opposite it.

"Bienvenue a mes amis," said Francois, who then repeated his greeting in English, "Welcome, my friends!"

"Thank you, Francois. We are excited to learn from you today!" said Sarah before introducing everyone.

"Well it's certainly so nice to meet all of you, and I'm thrilled to once again be reunited with my friend, Sarah. Now that you have come to Crofton, we're practically neighbors," declared Francois.

"I know, it's so great to see you, Francois, and I'm excited to have the opportunity to work with you again!" exclaimed Sarah.

"Okay, well enough reminiscing let's go throw some paint onto the walls." Their teacher laughed.

"Ladies, please pick your workstations. There's an easel set up for each of you with everything you'll need, including a pair of plastic gloves that you'll want to put on before we begin. Oh and, Sarah, would you please join me up here in the front of the room. I'm going to make you my helper today," said Francois.

"Absolutely, Francois!" said Sarah.

Tricia quickly identified her area and then picked up the linen tool and began brushing her long blonde hair with it. "Hey, guys, look at me. How do you like my new brush?"

"Oh brother, what, are we in kindergarten?" mumbled Brittany under her breath.

"Actually that's called a wall weaver brush, and it's what we'll be using today to create the technique. In fact, next to your easel you'll also find some white satin latex paint, a container of pearl glaze, a roller with a 3/8-inch cover, painter's tape and some paper towels.

"Notice the large clip attached to your board; that will hold your practice sheet in place, so you don't have to worry about it slipping off. If you'd like you can use the tape to create a border around your paper. It's not necessary, but I thought I'd give you the option. It's really for taping off all the areas in the room where you don't want to apply the finish.

"Alright then, let's get started. The first thing you need to do is roll the base coat on. Typically, you would let that dry overnight, but we are going to speed up the process by using these hair dryers that Sarah is passing out," Francois said.

Once the samples were all dry, Francois continued, "Now you need to roll on the pearl glaze over the basecoat. You'll notice that the glaze doesn't dry as fast as regular paint thereby allowing us the time needed to go back and create the desired texture."

"Oh no, I think I put on too much. It's dripping onto the floor," said Tabatha.

Jackie leaned over to take a look. "Oh yuck, Tabatha, please promise me you're not going to do that when you work on my walls," she pleaded.

"Don't worry, Jackie, that's what drop cloths are for." Sarah giggled.

"Now, ladies, I'd like you to pick up your brush holding the bristles parallel to the surface, and then drag the brush down through the wet glaze. Work from top to bottom, holding the bristles of the brush against the surface with the handle tilted slightly toward you. This keeps the bristles rigid, creating the streaked look. You're going to want to wipe the excess glaze from the brush after each downward pass to ensure a dry brushing surface.

"When you're finished you'll need to pass over your work again with the dryers. But when painting a room be sure to allow the glaze to dry on its own."

Once they were finished drying the boards, Francois continued "Now ladies it's time to apply a new coating of glaze. Then using your brush once again drag the walls, but this time horizontally, from left to right. One of the most important things to remember when you're working on a large wall is to section them off into about three- or four-foot areas. This way the glaze doesn't have a chance to dry before you're finished," instructed Francois.

"Yeah, I know you said the glaze takes longer to dry than just regular paint but it still dries a little too fast for me or I just need to work faster," laughed Jackie.

"Wow, look at mine, guys. Do you like it?" asked Maggie.

THE DECORATING CLUB

"It's beautiful!" said Francois. "But keep in mind you still have another hour to practice before I have to kick you all out. So please grab another sheet and do it again."

The last hour flew by, and the members became much more confident in their newly developed skill.

"Well done, ladies, you all did a wonderful job," said Francois as he looked around the room.

"Thank you so much for teaching us. I had a great time," said Reshma.

"Yes it was fun and a lot easier than I was expecting it to be," said Jackie.

"I agree," said Tabatha.

"I'm so glad. I knew you guys would enjoy it," said Sarah.

"How about you, Brittany? You're awfully quiet. Don't you have anything to say?" asked Tricia.

"Yeah, help me get these stupid gloves off. I don't want to wreck my manicure!"

"Okay, on that happy note, thank you again, my friend," Sarah said as she leaned in to give Francois a kiss on both his cheeks.

SUSAN M. MEYERS

* * *

The Cream Tea

*There was something about that restaurant that
brought happiness to my soul,
Perhaps the warm scones and clotted cream or
hanging pots and bowls.
Maybe the little ladies who called us love and dear.
But the thought of never going back again was
becoming a growing fear.
So there's now a room within our home once
underused and filled with clutter,
That's been magically transformed into a new
"Cream Tea"... perhaps even better.*

* * *

The boys' room would be repurposed to serve as Jackie's new office. Her intention was to recapture the feeling and atmosphere she enjoyed years ago in that special little English café. The team listened with great interest as Jackie described her vision for the room based upon all her wonderful memories.

"It was the cutest little place, and I can see every detail in my mind's eye as if it was just yesterday. I was in a small sea town in the south of England, near Cornwall. All the streets were cobble stone and filled with quaint little shops. On one of them was a small restaurant named the Cream Tea Café. It looked very welcoming and had a hand-painted picture of a teapot over the doorway.

"Since it was way past lunchtime and I was starving I decided to step inside. When I opened the door, I was overwhelmed by the amazing smell of freshly baked scones.

"A sweet little old lady then led me to my table. I remember she wore a neatly pressed floral apron and a matching bonnet in her hair.

"The table was round and clothed in maroon taffeta with a bright white lace overlay. A huge antique wooden cabinet sat opposite of me and was filled with all different pretty bone china tea sets.

"There were several hand-painted menu boards hanging on each of the stained oak-paneled walls that listed the featured specials of the day as well as a wide array of loose-leaf tea blends. There was a rustic-looking ledge about six feet up from the floor that encircled the room and placed on it were tons of jam and jelly jars.

"In one corner of the room was a painted picture of the British flag displayed in an old cracked glass frame. Oh, and you should have seen the ornate crystal chandelier that hung in the center of the room; it was stunning.

"All and all, the eclectic mixture of countryside and elegance gave way to a quaint, warm and inviting atmosphere."

"Wow, what a memory!" said Tabatha.

"Yeah, I remember everything about it! The best part, though, was when I was sitting there enjoying my tea and scones and all of a sudden the most handsome man I'd ever seen was standing in front of me asking if he could join me at the table—and that was when I first met the love of my life."

"Oh, how romantic!" Maggie interrupted.

"Yes," Jackie said as she continued. "Now maybe you guys can understand why I want my office to reflect the original Cream Tea Café."

* * *

Now that the room designs were more or less set, the Decorating Club had a much clearer picture of where they were going. Based upon what Jackie had shared, the team concluded that while they could readily handle painting and accessorizing, a big part of Jackie's answer to her "How am I going to get there?" question would involve work performed by outside help including carpenters, sheet rockers and electricians.

But, the first step was for Jackie and Steve to set a budget. Once that was established, Brittany teamed with Jackie to obtain and contrast job proposals. Then once the work began, they continued their collaboration by sharing the role of general contractor and worked together to oversee the project from start to finish.

Finally, a few weeks later, when most of the work had been completed, the girls all met up again. This time it was for a shopping trip to venture out in search of furniture and accessories.

"Wow, Jackie, everything looks amazing!"

"Yeah, things are really shaping up."

"Thank you, honestly I owe a lot to Brittany. First, she helped me get all the estimates for the work, and then she's been here to make sure everything was done right. I couldn't have done it without her."

"Well that's nice, but the truth is, if there's one thing I'm good at it's telling men what to do." Brittany laughed.

"Ha ha, that's very funny," said Reshma quietly.

"Jackie has the project stayed pretty close to budget thus far?" asked Sarah.

"Yes, Sarah, it has. In fact, I'm crossing my fingers that we'll be under budget now that everyone is helping. I mean wouldn't it be amazing if there was enough left over to go on another trip back to England," teased Jackie.

"Yeah, but forget going with Steve; you should take all of us; your worker bees. Besides, maybe we can finally go curtsy with the queen after all," joked Tricia.

"Ugh, you don't curtsy with the queen! God help England!" said Brittany as she lowered her head into her hand.

"Excuse me, ma'am, but is this about where you want the chandelier to hang?" asked Rocky, the electrician.

"Yes, I think that looks good, Rocky. What do you think, Sarah?" asked Jackie.

"Yes, I think that's perfect! Now we just need to go find a round table to go underneath it."

Sarah then picked up her keys and purse and headed towards the door. "Alright, guys, let's get going."

"Yes," said Jackie, "let the accessory shopping begin!"

The girls all piled into Sarah's green minivan and headed towards Annapolis.

"So does anyone have anything special planned for this weekend?" asked Maggie.

"Well, David is going to China and leaves Friday, so I'm planning on flying down to Georgia for the weekend," said Brittany.

"What's in Georgia?"

"Are your kids going too?"

"Wow, he sure travels a lot."

"Why China?"

"Yes, he does. I don't know, something about it being one of the countries representing the largest portion of the global banking sector . . . blah, blah, blah . . . ICBC blah, blah . . . CCB blah, blah and more BLAH."

"No, the kids are NOT going! Consuela will watch them. I'm going to my favorite spa, Chateau Elan Winery & Resort and I will be spending the weekend in a robe and slippers while being fed grapes," she laughed.

"Oh, lovely," said Maggie. "I wish someone would pamper me like that. I haven't had a facial or a massage in years."

"Oh, honey, you need to live a little," said Brittany.

"Honestly I think I'm way past the facial stage. That's great for younger women, but there's no miracle jar that's going to be able to fix this face," said Maggie.

"What, are you kidding me? You're beautiful, Maggie!" said Sarah.

"Ah, bless your heart, you're so sweet. What are you doing this weekend, Sarah?"

"Well on Saturday I'm going to be presenting at a seminar in Annapolis..."

"Oh wow! What is it about?" asked Tabatha.

"It's on the importance of staging your home to compete in today's real estate market," said Sarah

"Staging your home?" asked Reshma. "I'm not sure I understand."

"Well simply put, I'm just going to talk about how to make a home look more attractive to future suitors," said Sarah.

"That's cool Sarah but how do you do that?" asked Reshma.

"To be honest, it's basically the opposite of what we are doing right now with all of your homes. Instead of telling about a homeowner's unique story within their walls, a staged home is neutralized in such a way that it doesn't share any story.

Thus making it more attractive to prospective buyers who in the end only want to visualize themselves living there and not the current owners," explained Sarah.

"Well, I guess that makes sense. I mean unless someone met their husband in the same way and in the same place I did, they might not appreciate having the

Cream Tea in one of the rooms of their home," offered Jackie.

"I don't know I still think it's kind of cool. I mean after all, it gives you an excuse to enjoy yummy scones whenever you want and I'd certainly be up for that," laughed Maggie.

It was around lunchtime, and the girls were having no luck finding the things on Jackie's list.

So, to prevent Reshma from "falling on the floor if I don't eat something soon," they decided to stop off for a quick bite to eat and then raced back to Home Goods in the Waugh Chapel Towne Center.

"Hey guys look over here. Isn't this the cutest little table–and with these two matching chairs I can just visualize myself sitting with my clients while enjoying some tea and scones? What do you think?"

"I think they're adorable," said Maggie.

"Yes, I like them very much too," said Reshma.

"I agree I think they'll be perfect – but what about when you're not with your clients? Is there some other kind of furniture you might like to incorporate into the room as well?" asked Sarah.

"What do you mean like a sofa or a coffee table?—because I really don't want to take away from it looking like the café," said Jackie as she tried to understand what Sarah meant.

"No, I just thought maybe you'd like a comfy chair that perhaps could sit in another corner of the room out of the way and maybe a little table next to it where you could put your office phone on top of," offered Sarah.

"Oh you're right I love that idea, good thinking Sarah!" exclaimed Jackie.

"Hey guys look what I found," said Tricia as she approached the other members.

"Look it's a picture of a British flag. I found it in the sale section because it has a little crack in the glass. Talk about a perfect coincidence, right?"

"Yes Tricia that's absolutely perfect!" said Jackie.

It was approximately 2:15 when the girls wheeled their carts overfilled with shopping bags to the van. The contents included jam and jelly jars, boxes of scone mix, two pretty floral pillows, a wool throw, curtain rods, two thick chair pads in pink and maroon check and several un-chalked chalkboards. The larger items, including a beautiful brown leather chair with a matching ottoman and a cream-colored area rug would be delivered to Jackie later that week.

The look of the authentic Cream Tea Café was now in the works. But, Jackie wanted her clients to experience it through all of their senses just as Sarah had mentioned while describing her 3D design approach.

"Hey, guys, I forgot to tell you, but I remembered hearing something funny when I first walked into the Cream Tea back then," said Jackie.

"Oh cool, what was it?" asked Sarah.

"It was the sound of little birds chirping, and I found a tape that sounds exactly like it. I thought I could play that as background music," said Jackie.

"You even remembered the way it sounded, are you kidding me?" asked Tricia.

"Yes, Tricia, I told you I remember everything about it," said Jackie.

"Well that's awesome that you found one. Now you're surely hitting all the senses." Sarah giggled.

"You're right! Oh, and you know what else? I'm so excited because I'm finally going to be able to take my beautiful china out of storage that I purchased in England. Believe it or not I've never even used it," admitted Jackie.

"Ah, that's great! I bet you never thought you'd be christening it like this though, you know - in your own cafe," said Tabatha.

"Yeah, I'm looking forward to incorporating it into the room design. I think it really adds to the authenticity. Ha ha besides I'm not the best baker so I'm hopeful my beautiful china will carry me through and make my scones taste even better," laughed Jackie.

The Party

It was the first time Sarah and the rest of the Decorating Club would meet in a social setting with their spouses. The girls were all very excited about being together and proud to show their husbands all they had accomplished.

Maggie and Mark were the first ones to arrive, with the aroma of Old Bay seasoning trailing behind. Maggie had made her much-celebrated special crab dip recipe for the occasion and wanted to put it in Jackie's oven to keep warm.

The rest of the members were not far behind, and soon a steady procession was barreling through the front door. Within a matter of minutes, Jackie's kitchen was full of her fellow members and their better halves all buzzing about the topic of the night.

"Well, how did it feel to be the first victim?" Mark asked as he stretched out his hand to Steve.

"I won't lie; I was a little nervous at first, but I couldn't be happier. Not only is the Decorating Club responsible for redesigning our two rooms, they also helped Jackie redesign her life. And now with all the extra income I'm anticipating, I've actually started to think about retiring," joked Steve. "Thanks to the beautiful woman who let me sit down in a little café just like this one," he told the group as he waved his arm around Jackie's office, "and to whom I'm eternally grateful didn't just tell me, 'Beat it, mate!'"

"Wow, how sweet. I wish my husband thought about me that way," Maggie softly said as she reached for another potato chip.

While it seemed Maggie thought she was having the conversation in her mind, Sarah, who was standing next to her, clearly heard the painfully uttered words.

Jackie just shook her head and smiled at Steve's comment. Retiring was something that Jackie could never see for her husband. Steve loved being a pediatric dentist and had shown no signs of ever retiring. He was tall in stature, quite handsome and resembled a British aristocrat. A very energetic fifty-six-year-old who, besides his love for work, had other passions including his family, weight lifting, and of course, at the top of his list, Jackie.

All in all, the evening was a huge success. Everyone had a wonderful time, and it was obvious that a natural bond was beginning to form as the couples were starting to feel quite comfortable around each other. Even so, no one appeared anxious to ask the big question. Then as if on cue, Eric, Tabatha's husband, made the move: "So, whose house is next?"

"Well if it's alright with Maggie and Mark, I was thinking that their house could be next," said Sarah.

"That would be great," Maggie quickly replied as she glanced over at Mark. "You'll just have to tell your boss his wings are clipped when it's our time to host the Decorating Club cocktail party." The room went silent as they struggled to understand Maggie's comment.

Seeing the look of puzzlement on their faces, Mark volunteered, "Oh, didn't Maggie tell you, I'm one of the pilots for Air Force One."

CHAPTER 11

Don't Settle

Project #2—Maggie

Where am I?

TWO WEEKS LATER, the girls reunited to start their next project, this time at the home of Maggie and Mark.

"Welcome, everyone. Come on in," said Maggie as she opened the front door of her home.

"So before we get started on Maggie's project, I was hoping I could share some really big news with all of you," said Jackie.

"Sure, Jackie, what is it?" asked Sarah.

"Well first of all it seems like word of our little club is getting out."

"Why? What do you mean?" asked Tricia.

"Well Steve's brother came over yesterday with my sister-in-law to check out the café and workroom, and well of course they loved it. But, they also loved the whole concept of the club, and they talked it up last night while out at a dinner party. Anyway, one of the guests works at a news station, and they said they're going to pitch the idea about possibly doing a story on us in the future."

"Wow, that would be so cool," said Tabatha.

"Yeah, but I don't know if I want to be on TV," said Maggie.

"Why not?" asked Tricia.

"Because they say TV adds ten pounds on you, and I don't want to look fatter than I am," said Maggie.

"Oh, Maggie, stop," said Tabatha.

"And the other exciting news is there was also a couple there who have a daughter that is engaged, and, well, now I have my first client meeting set up for next week!"

"Congratulations, Jackie!"

"How exciting!"

"Good for you!"

"I'm so happy for you!"

"Will you remember us little people when you're rich and famous?"

"That's awesome!"

"Thanks, guys, but to be honest I am a little nervous. It's been a long time since I've actually worked on a gown, and to top it off the bride wants me to design a traditional Indian wedding dress. So, Reshma, I was hoping maybe before we leave today I could talk to you for a little bit and see if you had any suggestions for me," Jackie said as she put her hands together in a pleading gesture.

"Oh I'm so sorry, Jackie, but I don't think I can help you. It's been a while since I've been home, and I really don't remember what the dresses looked like. I'm sorry," said Reshma.

"When did you leave, when you were two?" countered Tricia.

"No, but to be honest I don't think about my homeland or its traditions or customs too often anymore," said Reshma.

Breaking the awkward silence, Maggie offered, "Well why don't we go in the kitchen now and have some coffee?"

"Sounds good to me!" said Sarah.

The girls had barely passed through the hall and into Maggie's kitchen when Brittany suddenly exclaimed

"What is that amazing smell?"

"Well it could be the banana bread, or the pumpkin nut muffins, or the chocolate chip scones. Unless, of course, you smell my famous shortbread," Maggie proudly said with a smile.

"Oh my gosh, Maggie, you've baked for an army. You didn't need to do all of that!" exclaimed Sarah as she quickly located the coffee pot and poured herself a cup.

"Oh, I didn't mind, Sarah. I love to bake," said Maggie.

"Yeah, there must be a zillion calories on this table. I can't eat any of this. I'm on a diet!" declared Brittany.

"Oh please, you on a diet?" questioned Maggie. "You look anorexic. You don't need a diet; you need to eat. I'm the one who needs to be on a diet!" Maggie said angrily.

"No you don't, Maggie. You look fine," responded Brittany.

"Fine??? You're being so sarcastic and mean!!! After all, we all have eyes here, don't we? Maggie does need a diet and if she doesn't lose weight soon she's going to get sick and end up at Anne Arundel Medical Center where she'll run right into me. That is, if she doesn't lay off the donuts," sniped Tricia.

"Me! How can you be so mean?" fired back Brittany

Maggie's face became red and blotchy and her eyes welled up with tears. "No, she's right; I am fat and I hate myself." Her lip quivered as she continued, "I'm useless and even my daughter thinks I'm a joke." Maggie took the tissue out of her pocket and wiped her nose. "And I'm sure if my husband hasn't had an affair yet he soon will be," cried out Maggie.

"Ouch!" thought Sarah as she tried to figure out a way to turn the situation from a negative into a positive.

But, before she had a chance to speak, Tricia jumped in and said, "What do you mean your daughter thinks you're a joke?"

"I think she's embarrassed by me. She says it's no wonder I'm fat; I eat junk food instead of superfoods. And when I asked her if she meant I needed to eat kryptonite, she just screamed, 'You're hopeless,' and slammed the door," said Maggie through her tears.

The room went silent. No one wanted to be the first to speak or even knew what to say.

Maggie wiped the tears from her eyes. She knew Tricia was right. In fact, her doctor had been telling her the same thing for months now. Only he did it in a much more kind and eloquent manner. Yet somehow, the way Tricia said it seemed to finally get through to her.

"Well this is kind of embarrassing. I mean you all came here to help me with my house, not to watch me stand here blubbering all day. I'm sorry; I don't know where all of that came from. I guess deep down I feel like I've lost who I was. My life used to be so different. I was young, thin, beautiful and ready to take on the world. Now I'm just old, fat, wrinkled and worthless."

"Oh, come on, Maggie. That's not true," said Tabatha.

"Yes, it is. There was a time once when Mark couldn't keep his hands off me. We were constantly going out to dances and parties, and he looked at me as if I was his princess. Now the only time it seems he notices me is when I'm putting something in my mouth. Then he says, 'Are you sure you want to eat that?'

"To make matters worse, it's pretty sad when you're only child doesn't even want anything to do with you. Yet I can't blame her, I don't even want anything to do with me.

"Well that's that, and if you guys want to leave, I'll totally understand," said Maggie.

"Maggie, nobody wants to leave. You're our friend, and friends help friends. Regardless, of whether the help is with a decorating project or with a life project, we're all here to provide support!"

"That's right, Sarah! We care about you, Maggie, and we want to help," said Brittany softly.

"Please don't be sad, Maggie," said Reshma.

"Yeah, we've got this! How can we help?" added Tricia.

"Aww, thank you so much. That means a lot to me, and, yes, I would appreciate all of your help," replied Maggie. "But honestly I don't even know where to start," she half-heartedly added. What do you think Sarah?

"Well for one I disagree with you, Maggie. Of course, you know where to start. You always need to start from where you are. It's the basic principle behind the need for knowing the answer to the first planning question: 'Where Am I?'

"In fact, when I'd meet my clients back in New Jersey, one of the first questions I'd ask them is, how long do you intend to live here? That would give both of us a sense of how much money and work they were willing to put into their redo. So, Maggie, I have a question for you. How long do you want to live here? And to be clear, I am not just talking about your house!

"If it's not a very long time, then you might get by with just rearranging the 'furniture' a little bit and hanging some new pictures. But if you want to live longer, then you'll need to address some of the things that are outdated and perhaps no longer work for you."

"I don't know, Sarah that sounds easier said than done," Maggie cautiously replied.

"I know change isn't always easy. But one approach that I've found helpful is based on the principle embedded in what I call the 'big black bag strategy,'" Sarah replied.

"Ha ha, that sounds like a tongue twister," commented Tabatha.

"You're right. It's hard to say, but the concept is easy to understand. The strategy is all about removing the clutter junking up our lives. Whether it's in our basement, our attic, our garage or throughout the whole house, most of us have some form of clutter. We even have it in our schedules and other parts of our lives as well as in our thinking. You know Maggie, removing the bad or negative things so we can focus on the good and positive things in our lives.

"The point is each type of clutter tends to prevent us from moving forward with what's important to us—causing us to get stuck in the mud. In fact, sometimes it seems like the things of least importance in life are the ones that weigh us down the most. We often tend to hang on to them and try 'decorating' around them, but sooner or later we realize that doesn't work. So, I believe every once in a while, you just need to get out the box of big black trash bags and dump the things that no longer work, making room for the ones that do," said Sarah.

"Yeah, Maggie, look at what happened to me. Now I can't imagine what my office and workroom would have looked like if I kept all the kids' stuff in there and just tried decorating around them," volunteered Jackie.

"Well, I bet that was a little more than you were expecting when you asked me what I thought Maggie, but I hope it was helpful. Why don't you sleep on it tonight and let's all reassemble tomorrow at the new health bar in town? They have a kale smoothie that I've been dying to try," said Sarah.

* * *

In a blink...

In time, paper peels, paint chips and furniture becomes worn-out and saggy. It's hard to recognize the onset of those ten extra pounds, just as it can be to foresee going from happy and positive to miserable and negative.

* * *

* * *

That night, Maggie reflected on the day and all the advice she received. She wondered how she got to this point in her life and why there were so many roadblocks preventing her from moving forward. Eventually, Maggie came to realize her insecurities had been stepping in the way of her relationships. It also became painfully clear that if she didn't overcome them and change her mind set things would never get better between her and her family.

Later, in the dark of night, Maggie awoke to a sobering realization.

CHAPTER 12

A New Day

Where Am I Going?

"GOOD MORNING, TEAM!" said Maggie cheerfully as she stepped through the door at Raven's Rafters and joined the rest of the Decorating Club members seated at the juice bar.

"Well it looks like someone got a good night's sleep," commented Tricia.

"Actually, no, I didn't sleep much at all. In fact, I had a very bad dream and couldn't go back to sleep after that."

"Oh, I'm sorry," said Reshma. "I hate when I have a bad dream too!"

"Yeah, it was wild and so vivid. I dreamt I was a little girl again, back in my mother's kitchen. The walls were covered with this disturbing wallpaper illustrated with pictures of all sorts of animals, like cows, pigs, turkeys, chickens and even some fish. Mixed in amongst the pictures were the words, 'You are what you eat!'

"I remember how scary it was as a kid because they weren't your friendly cartoon-type characters. Instead, I felt that they looked more like violent criminals staring down at me from wanted posters, as if I were eating one of their relatives.

"Anyway, last night, in my dream, they all came alive. They were very mean and frightening and started chasing me around my mother's kitchen as they chanted, 'You are what you eat, you are what you eat, you are what you eat...'

"Finally, around 2:00 a.m., I awoke in a cold sweat, and as I was wiping the sand out of my eyes, I spotted the plate of barbeque ribs on my night table that I brought with me to bed for a midnight snack. As I stared at the remains and thought about my dream, I came to the realization that I had to change the way I eat. So right then and there, I made up my mind to do just that.

"I spent the next several hours on my laptop searching the internet to find out what it had to say about the healthiest eating habits. I then used what I learned to design my own diet strategy and put together my first few healthy meals."

"Wow, that's great, Maggie!" exclaimed Tabatha.

"Yeah it actually was a lot of fun, and I'm very excited about my new approach. It will consist of five little meals that I'll strategically eat throughout the day, based upon the premise that I'll need fuel to keep my fire burning. Of course, the key is to choose the right fuel, and that should include a combination of fruits, vegetables and healthy proteins. I'll also modify my carb intake and work to exclude the empty calories by limiting my use of processed sugar.

"But the most important part of my strategy for taking back control of my life came to me just before the birds started chirping. Suddenly I realized the connection between what I eat and what I think. If we are what we eat, I reasoned we are what we think.

"Excuse me, are you ladies ready to order?" asked the clerk behind the counter.

"Please give us just a few more minutes. Go ahead, Maggie, continue," said Sarah.

"Well, I guess it's no secret that I haven't been thinking too highly or positively about myself lately, and last night I thought about what you said, Sarah, concerning the need to focus on the good and positive things in my life rather than the bad or negative ones. In other words, focus on what really matters.

"I came to realize that by doing that I'd naturally eliminate the things that don't really matter or just weigh me down, all the things that prevent me from achieving my goals. So, at five o'clock this morning I took your advice. I got a big black bag out and emptied my entire refrigerator and pantry of all the bad and empty calorie food into it. Then I went a step further, and I took a piece of paper and a pen and wrote down all of the negative and self-limiting beliefs I had about myself, including the things I've been doing to sabotage my relationship with my daughter. Then I crumpled the paper up and tossed it into the bag along with the rest of the garbage!"

"Wow, that's wonderful!" the girls seemed to exclaim in unison, amazed at Maggie's overnight transformation.

"I'm so proud of you," said Sarah. "It takes a lot of courage to look deep into the mirror and remove what you don't like seeing anymore. But, remember that's just half the job! Now that the 'room is swept clean', it's crucial for you to fill up the empty space left behind with the good and positive attributes, patterns and textures that will ensure your success," cautioned Sarah.

"Black bags, furniture, diets, relationships. . . I'm confused," Tricia groaned. "What are we talking about here, redesigning our homes or our lives?"

"It looks like a little bit of both," Sarah replied with a smile.

How am I going to get there?

The Decorating Club took a few weeks off to enjoy winter break with their families. Since the schools were closed, Tabatha and Eric decided to introduce their twin grandsons to the magic of Disney World. Brittany and David fled to the French Riviera with their three children, while the rest of the members enjoyed the holidays close to home.

By the time they all got back together, Maggie had already made huge strides with both her diet and her new way of thinking. She was celebrating her fifteen-pound mark and marveling at how much extra energy she was enjoying. So much so that she even joined in on one of her daughter's Zumba classes, sharing that she had never had so much fun.

Maggie was spending less time grazing in front of her refrigerator and more time experimenting in her kitchen perfecting her growing list of healthy recipes. At the same time, she was building a greater relationship with her daughter, Daniella who now instead of being embarrassed by her mom, was actually proud of her. Together they frequented book and health food stores where they learned more and more about the power of superfoods.

Whir, whir, whir . . .

"What is that loud noise?" asked Tricia as she entered Maggie's kitchen.

"Oh, I hope you guys don't mind, but I've replaced the usual face of our 'fuel' today with a healthier option," Maggie said proudly and loudly while trying to be heard over the buzz of the juicing machine.

"I'm in," yelled most of the girls, who were happy that the holidays were finally over and anxious to get back on track with their own diets.

"This is delicious!" remarked Tricia.

"Excuse me, what did you say, Tricia?" said Sarah in a shocked voice.

"I said this is delicious!" repeated Tricia.

"Well thank you," said Maggie.

"Tricia, are you feeling okay?" Sarah continued.

"Yes, I'm feeling okay! Why?" Tricia growled.

"Oh, nothing. You just don't seem like yourself." Sarah giggled and then continued, "Well it's good to see everybody again. I hope you guys all had a great time off."

"Yeah it was good, but to be honest I think I need another vacation from my vacation! I'm so exhausted, and for the life of me, no matter how hard I try, I can't get

'It's a Small World after All' out of my head!" joked Tabatha.

"Ha, ha I remember it took me a whole month the last time we went down there with our kids," laughed Jackie.

"Well, Maggie, did you have a chance to think about what room you want to work on and whether you've decided upon a vision for it?" said Sarah.

"Yes, yes, I did," said Maggie excitedly. "Over the break, I had a chance to sit down with Mark and Daniella. We decided the one room in our home that has the greatest potential and really serves no purpose is our basement."

"Although it's already a finished basement, it's currently just housing a bunch of junk." Maggie stopped for a second and glanced over at Sarah, then quietly said, "Or in other words, a bunch of outdated useless items that I no longer want to hang onto or decorate around. Instead, I want to turn our basement into a professional dance studio where Daniella and I plan to teach Zumba to other mothers and daughters."

"Wow, that's certainly a big change! So she doesn't think you're a joke anymore?" questioned Tricia.

"No, thankfully. She apologized for the way she's treated me in the past and explained that she was just worried about me. We've actually gotten very close lately. In fact, it turns out we even have a lot more in common than we knew. I guess it just took us spending more time together," said Maggie.

"That's beautiful. I'm so happy for the two of you. Life's too short not to get along," said Tabatha.

"Thanks, Tabatha, you're absolutely right."

"We're actually hoping our collaboration will inspire other mothers and daughters to spend more time with each other. Daniella feels that a lot of her friends at school and their moms might be interested."

"Well I think there's mothers and daughters even outside of her school that might be interested," volunteered Tricia.

"I hope so! Now I guess our next big challenge is just getting the word out," said Maggie.

"You should join the Crofton Chamber. That was the first thing I did when I started my business and believe me it really helped. I got three brides as a result," said Jackie.

"Oh, that's great. Thanks, Jackie, I'll have to look into that."

"Boy, this juice is amazing, Maggie. What's in it?" asked Sarah.

"Thanks, Sarah. I'm glad you like it. That's our other exciting news: Daniella and I have been creating healthy smoothie concoctions because we're planning to have a juice bar down there as well."

"In fact, Mark has been doing a lot of research on it and has identified one similar to the one in the White House."

"Wow, that's so cool, Maggie!" said Tabatha.

"Yeah, that sounds very exciting, Maggie, but do you have enough space?" asked Sarah.

Maggie smiled, and then replied, "Well, Mr. Mark seems to think so. He's been down there each night after work taking a bunch of measurements and said we should be good to go. Come on, let's go downstairs and I'll show you the space."

As the team moved to the lower level, they were surprised at how big the room was and just how perfect it would be for their newly energetic friend's vision. Although, it was obvious a lot of the clutter would have to be removed first.

"I know we will need to rip up the carpeting and replace it with a dance floor, and I was thinking of having an electrician put in a bunch of high hats 'cause it's very dark down here. Aside from that, though, the room itself is in pretty good shape. But I don't want our students to feel like they're just in a basement. Instead, I want them to feel like they're somewhere else, but where I don't know. Do you have any ideas, Sarah?" asked Maggie hopefully.

"Well I believe in every decorating project it's important to let the walls talk to you," said Sarah.

"Wait, talking walls? What did you put in her smoothie?" questioned Tricia.

"'Let the walls talk' is a phrase I adopted years ago and would say to each new client as we considered their space. A lot of them would look at me like I was some sort of mystical fortune-teller or way-out artist—kind of like Tricia is doing right now." Sarah smiled. "But others understood it as my need to take in and absorb what I was seeing and feeling and reflect on it. So, Maggie, if it's okay, I'm going to stay here a little while longer to listen to your walls and see if I can come up with a few possibilities. In the meantime, let's all meet back here again tomorrow, right after the bus leaves," Sarah replied.

* * *

For the next thirty minutes, Sarah walked around the room and reflected on what Maggie had shared about her vision. The words, "I want them to feel like they are somewhere else," kept repeating over and over again in her mind. While she strived to uncover clues for where Maggie's "somewhere else" could be, Sarah's mind drifted off to think about the word Zumba. "What does the word mean anyway and how and where did it start?" she thought. That night at home, Sarah went onto the internet to look for the answers.

During her search, Sarah discovered that the name Zumba comes from the Spanish verb zumbar meaning, "to buzz," "to whirr," or "to hum." Sarah came to understand that this was a reference to the very fast movements of a bee in flight and the buzzing sound made by their wings—in turn representing the two main elements of the exercise activity: fast movement and music.

Although Zumba was first introduced to the United States in Miami in 1999, the Latin-inspired dance class actually originated in Colombia more than a decade earlier. The concept of Zumba, dubbed a "dance party," grew out of an improvised dance class held in a Colombian aerobics studio during the '80s into a widespread exercise phenomenon boasting millions of regular participants.

As Sarah thought about the information she had accumulated, a few words popped out; Spanish, dance party and Colombia. "That's it," she thought. "I can see a dance party atmosphere that is portrayed through a relaxed Spanish Colonial sort of style—and we could mix in some of the Moorish influences that are often seen in Colombia."

Sarah got to work sketching potential layouts for the room and creating a storyboard filled with the colors, patterns and textures that represented the look. Her goal was to help Maggie design an area where her Zumba students would have fun and feel exhilarated and transfixed by a classy, elegant ambiance.

* * *

"That's beautiful," said Tommy as he glanced over Sarah's shoulder. "What's it for?" He moved in to take a closer look.

"Oh, these are some plans I'm working on for Maggie and Mark's basement. They want to turn it into a Zumba studio and have an area designated for a juice bar. The only problem is that with the fixed cost of the dance floor and the juicing setup, I'm concerned that there won't be enough left in their budget to hire a carpenter to build this dividing wall and the bar area," Sarah told him while pointing to the illustration.

"They're really going to have a Zumba studio? That's funny!" Tommy laughed.

"Why is it so funny?" asked Sarah.

"I don't know; I just had a vision of Mark jumping around in a pair of yoga pants, that's all."

"Well it's not going to be for Mark. It's going to be for Maggie and their daughter, Daniella, who plan on marketing it as a fun mother/daughter activity to other mothers and daughters," explained Sarah.

"Well, I think that's fantastic, and what great exercise! Hey, that reminds me; I went past that tennis shop in Annapolis the other day and saw a really pretty tennis skirt in the window. Do you want to go down on Saturday and take a look?" asked Tommy.

"No, thank you. I'm too busy right now to play tennis. Anyway, let me get back to this," said Sarah.

"Listen, Sarah, first of all, I'm very happy to see you once again embracing some of the things you're good at, but I also think it's important that you don't remain single focused. Let's face it; you do a lot around here: taking care of the kids, the house, now starting this club. That's a lot, not to mention taking care of me, and we know what a big job that can be." Tommy chuckled. "I want you to enjoy your life, and I know one of the things you always loved doing was playing tennis. You can't just turn your back on all the things that make you who you are. Besides, have I told you how hot you look in those little skirts?" Tommy said as he winked at Sarah.

Sarah got up from her desk walked over to Tommy and put her arms around his waist. Looking into his eyes, she said, "I love you, babe."

"I love you too, sweetheart. So does that mean we have a date to go to Annapolis on Saturday?" asked Tommy.

"Yes, under one condition. Promise me we'll stop off at Storm Bros and get a double, I mean triple scoop of moose tracks."

"Okay, miss, it's a plan. Oh, that reminds me I never got to the 'second of all,'" said Tommy.

"Second of all? What's a second of all?" asked Sarah.

"You know what a second of all is; it comes after a first of all! My second of all was to see if I could help out and if you think Mark and Maggie would be okay with that."

While Tommy worked Monday through Friday in the world of high finance, nothing made him happier than changing from work clothes into his T-shirt, jeans and tool belt on the weekends. They were the perfect team; whatever elaborate designs Sarah came up with, Tommy was always willing and able to create.

"Besides, why should you girls have all the fun? I'm sure I can get the guys to help me. Then we can share the limelight and have some pictures of us up there on the screen at the next Decorating Club . . . date," teased Tommy.

"Date?" questioned Sarah. "Don't you mean party?" she asked in a confused tone.

"No, I mean date as in you and me tonight—remember? We're supposed to go to that fundraiser you're involved in at Homestead Gardens," reminded Tommy.

"OH my gosh, I completely forgot," admitted Sarah. "I've got to get ready."

* * *

"Okay, guys, I'm going to need to focus on my list and what I have to get when we're inside so please be on your best behavior." said Sarah as she pulled into the Safeway parking lot the next day.

"Oh, oh, Mommy, are you going to give us our quarters?" asked Katie.

"Yes, Katie, I'll give you your quarters. Now please hold hands and let's get inside."

Sarah grabbed a cart from outside the grocery store and moved through the electric door with all four of her kids in tow.

"Okay guys; take your time and look at all of the machines before making your selections. I don't want you coming back until everyone's spent their quarters—and remember to stay together!" instructed Sarah.

"Onions, check; tomatoes, check; chop meat, check; cereal, check; milk, check; bread, check; pasta, check; dog food, check..."

"Hi, Sarah."

Sarah looked up from her list, "Oh, hi, Reshma, how's it going? Is this your little girl?"

"Yes, this is baby Lilly."

"Ah, Reshma, she's adorable!"

"Thank you." Reshma smiled and then continued, "So, Sarah, do you know yet when we are going to start back up at Maggie's house?"

"I'm hoping very soon. I know it seems like it's been forever. I'll have to call Maggie tonight so I can provide everyone with an update."

"Jackie told me it had something to do with the electric box. Is that right?" asked Reshma.

"Yes, unfortunately it did and it wasn't something they were expecting. I feel bad because they were so excited about the concept and layout I presented them with and wanted to move on it immediately. But the first thing they had to address was the lighting because it's was so dark down there. Yet when the electrician came to give an estimate, he noticed that water had gotten in from outside and rusted the circuit breakers. Then when he finally came back to replace the box, he realized a lot of the wires were faulty too, and I don't know Reshma; that's where it goes beyond my paygrade," said Sarah.

"What do you mean by paygrade? I don't understand," asked Reshma.

"Ha ha." Sarah giggled. "Well to put it very simply, I'm not smart enough to really understand more than that."

"Oh, I think that's a horrible word. I find you very smart," said Reshma.

Sarah smiled and then responded, "Thanks, Reshma, but not when it comes to electricity I'm not."

"Oh, I saw Maggie going into the post office the other day. I beeped at her but she didn't see me. Wow, Sarah, she really looks fantastic," exclaimed Reshma.

"I know. I think she said she's lost about a total of forty pounds. It's amazing, right? She's a walking billboard. I mean between perfecting her healthy smoothie recipes and choreographing her upcoming Zumba classes . . ."

"Excuse me, Sarah, but walking billboard?"

"Oh, sorry, Reshma. That just means she is portraying the image of good health. If you look at Maggie and see how she has been able to transform herself, she's showing the rest of us that we could do the same thing if we applied ourselves like she is," said Sarah.

"Hmm, that's what I've been trying to do, Sarah. I want to become an American billboard," said Reshma.

"You want to become an American billboard? I guess now I'm the one who doesn't understand, Reshma. Why do you want to be an American billboard?"

"Because I no longer live in India and I . . ."

"Hey, Mommy, we're back. Look what I got out of the bubblegum machine," Katie yelled excitedly.

"Katie, Miss Reshma was talking and you interrupted her. Please apologize," said Sarah.

"Oh no, Sarah, it's fine. I have to get going anyway. I'll talk to you soon," said Reshma as she wheeled Lilly down the grocery aisle.

CHAPTER 13

Hard Hat Zone

STANDING IN FRONT of Tommy, Anil raised his right hand in what appeared to be a saluting motion and said, "Good morning, sir, Anil Patel here reporting for duty."

Before Tommy had a chance to address Anil, Paul swooped in, also raised his hand, and said, "Morituri te salutant."

Tommy then returned the salute and said, "Okay, I give, what does that mean?"

"It's Latin for, 'those of us who are about to die salute you.' It was something the gladiators did out of respect for the emperor when they showed up for a day's work at the Colosseum in Ancient Rome."

His explanation sparked the rest of the men to follow suit.

"Ha ha, you guys are very funny. But this basement hardly looks like the Colosseum, and I'm not asking you to die, just lend a hand," said Tommy.

"Yeah, that may be true, but I noticed you didn't dispute the whole emperor title," joked Steve.

"Oh yeah, that's right: I'm the emperor, and you gang of misfits are my gladiators. Now throw on your gloves and let's get to work."

The first activity involved ripping up the carpeting and preparing the space for where the dance floor would be located. Next, the guys took a lot of measurements, each in turn emphasizing the importance of measuring twice. Then they pontificated, paced back and forth, argued over whether Home Depot or Lowes was the better big-box home improvement store and then finally decided to go on a field trip down Route 3 to visit both, "after all they have locations right across the road from each other," and were gone for what seemed like eternity. But, once they returned they busily got to work magically transforming the previously unused basement into a cute little dance studio.

Boom! Boom! Crash! Bang!

"Hey, take it easy over there! Let's not knock down everything we just put up!" said Tommy.

"Oh sorry, Tommy, that was me. I just bumped into the pile of extra wood," said Eric.

"That's it, no more beer for him!" teased Paul.

"So now that we've got the dividing wall up and the bar made, what's next, chief?" asked Mark.

"Hey! Don't forget my amazing keyhole archway over here. I think it's a masterpiece if I do say so myself."

"Yes, Anil you've done a great job, buddy," said Tommy.

"Thank you, thank you very much," Anil said in a deep voice.

First looking down at his watch and then in a tired raspy voice, he said, "I vote we call it a day. Besides, tomorrow the girls are going to use the white Venetian plaster over there to cover the walls, and then after it dries they want us to come back and burnish it. And my body needs some rest before that's happening," Tommy said as he picked up his jacket.

*　*　*

Ding-dong.

I'll be right there!" hollered Maggie.

Maggie put the folded laundry on the steps and then walked over and opened the front door.

"Oh hi, Sarah."

Looking at the large box in Sarah's arms, she asked, "Can I help? That looks heavy."

"No, that's okay, Maggie. I'll put it downstairs when we're done, but first I want to show you the mosaic tiles that just came in."

Sarah opened the box and began gently pulling out the tiles and placing them on the floor.

"Oh, thank goodness," she said in a relieved tone.

"Is there a problem?" asked Maggie.

"Not anymore. At first, I was worried they didn't include the spec sheet. And if that was the case we'd have no idea how to recreate the pattern."

"Phew, that would have been bad. You really think we can do this though, right? I mean, don't we have to cut some of the tiles to make them all work, and do we need to buy some kind of machine?"

"No, don't worry. Tommy has all the right tools, and he knows what to do. He actually learned while he was in Morocco."

"Morocco? When did he go there?"

"Oh, that was before he met me, during his young and carefree days. I didn't tell you he went backpacking around the world?"

"No! Wow, that's fascinating! I wish I could have done that when I was young and carefree!"

"Hey, Sarah, tell me again why they only create geometric designs with the tiles?"

"Oh, well I believe it's to represent the language of the universe and to help the believer to reflect on the infinity of God."

"But the tiles are also very popular in soothing environments and are often used as a backdrop for meditation, and, well, I thought that might be appropriate since your desire is to take your patrons to another place. That sounded funny, but you know what I mean."

"Ha ha, yeah, I know what you mean. But thanks, that's very powerful. Oh, and speaking of powerful, let me show you my new dress."

Maggie ran upstairs to her bedroom closet and moments later returned holding a figure-flattering ribbed black dress with a plunging neckline.

"What do you think, Sarah? I want to wear this to our cocktail party. Mark hasn't seen it yet, and I'm hoping it will make a powerful statement." Maggie laughed.

"Powerful statement? Forget that. I think you're going to leave the poor guy powerless! Maggie, the dress is beautiful, and again, you look absolutely amazing. I'm so happy for you."

"Thanks, Sarah. I have to say things definitely have changed for me, and for the better. I used to think the best years of my life were over. I didn't feel attractive anymore, and honestly I blamed it all on Mark." Maggie stopped for a second and then continued, "I felt like our marriage was stuck in first gear, but it wasn't him, it was really me. I was so unhappy with myself that I was pushing him away. But not anymore!"

Just then, Maggie broke out in song as she shuffled around the room. "I got knocked down and baby I got up again!"

* * *

The successful creation of the Zumba studio, complete with professional juice bar, represented the combined effort of many hands. While the couple experienced some unforeseen setbacks in the beginning, the new studio was now finally completed.

The members all came together in celebration, and as they sipped on drinks made from fresh fruit infused with vodka and rum, they were serenaded by Latin music echoing throughout the dance floor.

The party continued into the wee hours of the morning and was highlighted by a variety of candid shots of the newest members at work, a spirited Conga line and Maggie's very hot, sexy, size-8 dress.

CHAPTER 14

Date Night

"I TOLD KATIE it's my turn, right, Mom?" said Darcy.

"No, it's not, Darcy. You went two weeks ago. It's my turn," said Maddie.

"No I didn't. Collin went two weeks ago. Remember, they went go-karting?" said Darcy.

"Oh, yeah, well it's still not your turn, 'cause it's my turn," said Maddie.

"Mom, tell her it's my turn!" shouted Darcy.

"Come on, guys, stop fighting. Maddie is right; it is her turn. Now you guys behave for Daddy and go to bed when he says. Are you ready, Maddie? Let's go," said Sarah.

"Yes, Mom, I'm right behind you," she said. But first Maddie turned around to face Darcy and before sticking her tongue out as far it would go, said, "I told you so."

A short while later Sarah opened the door to the bead store and greeted the woman at the front desk.

"Hi, this is our first time here. I'm Sarah, and this is my daughter Maddie. We have very little experience, so I'm hoping you can tell us where to begin."

"Sure!" said the enthusiastic young woman. "So are you looking to make a gift for someone, or do you want to make something like a necklace or bracelet for yourselves, and are you both going to make something?" questioned the clerk.

"We're on a date, and we're both going to make something," fired back Maddie. "There's four of us, so my mom takes one of us out every week so we can do something special together, just by ourselves. Last week she took Katie out to a place where they learned how to make ice cream. Collin went go karting, and dumb Darcy who thinks she's sooo smart got to go meet her favorite author. But me, I'm the creative one, so we always do something creative when it's my turn, and today it's beads," Maddie said without coming up for air.

After picking all of their beads, the duo sat down at the long wooden table and listened to a young woman instruct them on how to make a necklace.

"Wow, this is kind of fun, isn't it, Mom?"

"Yes, Maddie, it is, and you're doing a beautiful job."

"Yeah, I really like all these colorful beads, but I didn't see any of the charms like what we get out of the bubble gum machine. I think I'd like to add one of those. Excuse me, but do you have any bubblegum?"

"Shh, Maddie, don't ask that. They won't have any of those here," said Sarah.

"So tell me what's going on with school. Did Mrs. Givens like your project?"

"Yeah, she thought it was pretty cool, but you know the green food coloring we used? Well, it kinda got on her dress, and she didn't seem too happy about that."

"Hey, Mom, do I have to go feed people? 'Cause I don't want to. Besides, I don't know why they can't just feed themselves. It's not like they're babies."

"Maddie, what are you talking about?"

"Oh, I overheard Mrs. Carbone, my Girl Scout leader, talking about our troop earning a badge by going to some shelter and feeding people."

"That's right, I did hear something about that. Maddie, of course you should go, but not because you have to, but because you want to. Serving others is a privilege not a chore. It's an opportunity to share who you are and what you do with others. It's an amazing feeling to put all of your own problems to the side and think about those who are in real need. Not everyone is as fortunate as we are. The things we worry about can't compare with what some other people have to deal with every day. After all, that's why we're here."

"Oh, is that why we moved to Crofton? Because you needed to help all the moms decorate their homes?"

"No! No! That's not why we moved to Crofton." Sarah stopped for a moment, her eyes filled up with tears. "Hmm, maybe that is why we're here."

CHAPTER 15

Be Courageous

Project #3—Tricia

Where am I?

"I WAS WONDERING if my home could be the next Decorating Club project," Tricia hesitantly said into the phone.

"Yes, of course. That'll be fine," replied Sarah. "Do you know what room you'd like to work on, and if so, do you have a vision for it?"

"Well, yes, I think I want to turn our spare room into a bedroom slash office for me," she added without emotion.

"Um, okay, Tricia, I'll gather the girls and we'll see you Wednesday morning," said Sarah, trying to sound upbeat.

* * *

Tricia and Paul both came from very large families. Tricia, the only girl, had six older brothers, while Paul, one of eight, had five brothers and two sisters. The couple had been married for seven years but had no children of their own.

Tricia worked very long shifts at the hospital and most nights slept on the couch. Being an operating room nurse exposed her to the hard side of life, especially witnessing the deaths of so many patients that in her mind could have been prevented if they had just taken better care of themselves.

Paul worked in a small advertising agency in Annapolis and left at five o'clock every afternoon, allowing him just enough time to run home, get changed and be on the field or in the gym, ready to coach one of his many youth sport teams.

Because of their work schedules and the stress of Tricia's job, the couple seemingly had been living separate lives.

THE DECORATING CLUB

* * *

Wednesday morning brought cloudy skies and torrential downpours for the Decorating Club members as well as the rest of Anne Arundel County. Given the nature of their next project, Sarah couldn't help but wonder if the stormy weather was reserved exclusively for the home they had just entered on Meadowbrook lane.

"I'm sure Sarah told all of you, but my redo is turning our spare room into a bedroom/office for me. Since I work so many crazy hours, I want to be able to come home and sleep straight through without being woken by the sounds of Paul getting ready for work. Besides, sometimes I can't sleep right away, so I read until I get drowsy and Paul inevitably complains that I'm keeping him awake.

"So I thought it might be best if I just sleep in a separate room. My plan is for it also to serve as my office, where I can work."

"I thought you worked at the hospital," said Reshma.

"Yes, I do, but I hate it. I'm so sick and tired of seeing sick people!" said Tricia.

"But isn't that why they come to the hospital?" asked Reshma.

"Yeah, but if they weren't so afraid of every little thing they wouldn't need to come to the hospital. I believe many of their health problems are a result of fear. If they focused on all the good in their lives and not all the bad they would be so much happier and healthier," said Tricia.

"W-H-A-T? Are you saying the hospital is filled with sick people because they don't think right? And if so, just what do you think you're going to do to change all of that?" asked Brittany.

"Yes, Brittany, that's exactly what I'm saying! You have to understand that some people are just like sheep being led around and spoon-fed lies or half-truths each day by social media, the news and advertisements. And how do they respond? They simply accept it; they submit and settle for less, just so they can fit in.

"My desire is to become a life coach and help people understand and resist how today's world uses fear to manipulate them."

"I know I'm still new to this country, but I don't understand. How do they do that?" asked Reshma innocently.

"Are you kidding me? It's everywhere. We're bombarded with it every day from every direction! Haven't you been paying attention? Or did you already forget what happened right here in our own backyard? We were all afraid to leave our houses for fear of being shot, by the DC sniper. It was all we heard about day and night," declared Tricia.

"But we were afraid and had every right to be afraid with all those people being shot. Ten innocent people died!" snapped Brittany.

"Okay, ladies, let's see the room," said Sarah in an effort to get them refocused.

While it was clear that Tricia had a lot of passion for helping people, 'wake up and smell the coffee', it was equally clear to Sarah that Tricia was masking her own pain and struggles. Sarah had mixed feelings about assisting her with what in Sarah's mind, would be a big mistake. Given the recent history, Sarah was afraid that separate sleeping quarters might be the last straw to knock an already shaky marital structure off its foundation.

* * *

Tricia led them down the hall to the spare room. "Wow, it's huge," said Sarah looking at the roughly 350 square feet in front of her. "Why haven't they used this as the master bedroom?" she wondered.

The walls of the room were painted white, and the floor was covered in tan wall-to-wall carpeting that looked like it had never been walked on. The only items in the room were an old rocking chair positioned in one of the corners and three big boxes on the floor next to it.

"I have an old full-size bed in the garage that I think we can use. It's from when Paul and I lived in Odenton. Our townhouse was very small, and nothing else fit. I also have an old desk out there from Paul's mother. He carved his name into it when he was a boy, and although his mom didn't have space for it, we held on to it because she didn't want it to go to the trash. So I can use that, since it's just sitting there anyway."

"What about that chair and the boxes, are those things you might like to incorporate into the design?" Sarah asked.

After a moment, Tricia responded softly, "No, they can go to the garage."

Tricia's mom once used the chair to cuddle her in as a small child while reading Tricia bedtime stories. It had been sitting in the room since the day they moved in. Now the chair along with the boxes filled with storybooks would be relocated to the garage.

"So what's your vision for this room, besides just adding those two pieces of furniture? Would you like some custom curtains, have you given any thought to accessories and lighting?" Sarah questioned. "No, I don't care. I have no sense of style; I'm good with whatever you decide," said Tricia.

"Whoa, Tricia, wait a minute," Sarah began. "While that may or may not be true, that was not part of the deal. I explained to all of you in the beginning that I believe a home should tell a story of the people who live there. I agreed to help, but not by reflecting my story in your home. It has to be your story!" Sarah re-emphasized.

"Well, my story is sad. In fact, I'm sorry I wasted all of your time. Let's forget it. I have to run now anyway—off to my stupid job, where I'll be for like the next hundred hours or so!" Tricia whined.

"What a hypocrite!" Brittany snipped. "You stand on a soapbox saying the rest of the world is paralyzed by fear, causing us not to live the lives we were intended to live. Yet there you are, running off to a job you clearly hate just because you're obviously too afraid to do something about it. I'm sick and tired of hearing you make belittling comments about others, when it's you, Tricia, who should be taking a long hard look in the mirror!"

"Oh boy, here we go again," thought Sarah as she watched closely to see who was going to throw the first punch.

"That's it! I quit! I quit! I QUIT!" repeated Tricia, getting louder each time. "Come on, Tricia, nobody wants you to quit. We're all friends here. Tempers are just running high today; I blame it on the weather. Let's all just take a deep breath and calm down," urged Sarah.

"No, I'm not calming down. I'm going to quit my job! Brittany is right! I hate my job and I feel stuck. I want to help others who feel the same way because I really believe I can make a difference. So that's it: I'm going to become a life coach—and I'm starting with me!

"This is something I've thought about for a long time, and I'm sick and tired of just talking about it. It's never going to happen unless I quit my job and have the courage to step out on my own—and today's that day!

"The first thing I'm going to do is complete my project plan and give special attention to the 'Who Am I?' section. I apologize to all of you, and if you'll agree to still help, I promise to be more prepared to share my vision at our next meeting and vow to be less of a jerk," Tricia said humbly.

"Wow, that's a big change, Tricia. Are you sure you don't want to sleep on it?" asked Maggie.

"Nope, I've never been surer," said Tricia confidently.

"Well I'll be happy to still help you, Tricia," said Reshma, followed by the rest of the members.

* * *

HELP!

*I'm being held captive by a kidnapper named Fear.
What he looks and sounds like is a mystery that's unclear
All I know is, he's captured my mind, heart and soul
And I have fallen deeply under his control.*

* * *

Where am I going?

The Decorating Club took the next eight weeks off as they waited for Tricia to finish out her notice at the hospital and have time to focus on developing her plan for a new life.

"It's so nice to see you guys again. Thanks so much for coming back and agreeing to help me with my project," Tricia said as she invited the girls in.

"Paul and I are so excited to finally be turning this empty room into something useful. In fact, we decided the space would best serve solely as an office for me to meet with my clients. There's no more need for an extra bed because I don't work crazy hours anymore," Tricia excitedly announced.

"That's great, Tricia, and you're going to love having your office right in your home. I know that at first I was nervous that my brides wouldn't take me seriously enough since it wasn't located in a storefront. But I can't tell you how many compliment the warm and inviting atmosphere you guys all helped me to create, and I'm sure we can do the same for you," said Jackie.

"Thanks, Jackie. Well this is my project plan and inspiration file. They're packed with ideas for the room," said Tricia proudly.

THE DECORATING CLUB

"That's wonderful. Thank you for being so well prepared. Now let's see what your story has to say," commented Sarah while opening the file.

Inside were six different shades of pink paint chips; eight different pink fabric swatches in various materials; a lace doily and about sixty pieces of paper each with a different, positive handwritten quote.

"Well," said Sarah, "it looks like you sure like pink, but I'm confused about the quotes."

"I do like pink," said Tricia. "I never thought I did, but I do! With six brothers, pink wasn't a color I saw too often. As you might guess, it was usually blue, although there were a lot of times when it was black and blue," she teased.

"Wait, oh yeah, I get it. That's funny. But what about the quotes?" chimed in Tabatha.

"Well I grew up in an entrepreneurial household. My brothers are self-employed, my dad is self-employed, his dad was self-employed, and his dad was self-employed. My father's brother is also self-employed; in fact, he's a multi-millionaire living in a huge mansion in Florida. I remember him coming up for a visit when I was a little girl for the sole purpose of sharing his secret for success with my dad.

"He stayed for a week or so, and every day he would spend hours talking to my father and my six brothers about the 'keys to success.' My uncle told them that if they read the books and listened to all the tapes he left for them; it would open the door to greatness.

"I remember asking my uncle, 'Can I walk through the door too?' Then my brothers told me, 'Beat it,' my father told me, 'Go find your mother,' and my uncle told me, 'No, little girl, this is only for men.'

"But I never forgot the last thing I heard him say to them as he left, 'Remember, no one can do it for you.'

"Years later, I found the books and tapes in an old cedar chest up in my parents' attic. It took months, but I read every book and listened to every tape, and eventually they became the guideposts for my life. Yet somewhere along the way, I began to lose my focus, first becoming distracted and finally frozen by fear.

"You guys helped me realize that and now I intend to take charge and regain my life. Although I mistakenly stopped following the timeless wisdom, I learned as a child, I'm determined to put it back into practice and now share it with other women. Wisdom, by the way, that is not reserved just for men.

"So I was thinking I'd like to paint the walls pink and give the room a very feminine feeling. Also, I thought it would be really cool if I had all these strong positive statements all over the walls!" said Tricia excitedly.

"I love it! We women have to stick together!" approved Jackie.

How am I going to get there?

Design Element—Wallcovering (Paint)

The painting committee's initial projects required learning faux finishes, first for Jackie's workroom and then again for Maggie's studio. But this time Sarah thought it might be helpful for the girls to spend a little time learning the basics of regular painting.

So she decided to approach Mr. Ditmar, a neighbor who lived a few houses down from her, with the idea of having him present a Painting 101 class to the members.

It so happened that Mr. Ditmar had retired from the secret service years ago. Unlike his peers, who pursued lines of work more consistent with their prior jobs after retiring, Ditmar sought employment at a local hardware store, where he now runs the paint department.

Mrs. Ditmar thought it was the perfect next step. "After all, he's painted every room in our home including the garage. Not to mention the outside of our house and the shed. We have nothing left!" she jokingly confessed.

SUSAN M. MEYERS

Painting 101

"Ladies, the first thing to remember is that sheen is important—and I'm not talking about Charlie!" chuckled Mr. Ditmar. "Nope, I'm talking about some other fellows named flat, matte, eggshell, satin, semi-gloss and high gloss. Each one of these guys has their own characteristics, and their performance plays a huge role in helping you achieve the overall look and feel that your project requires.

"For instance, high-traffic areas do well with gloss or satin because they hold up better to touching and can be cleaned more easily. But, beware! They also can make wall imperfections much more pronounced. I'm not sure what you ladies put on your face, but I know the misses uses some sort of light war paint to cover up whatever she doesn't like seeing—not that I think she needs to, but that's a story for another day. Heh, heh, heh.

"Just remember the more matte-like the finish, the fewer imperfections you'll see, but that also means the less durability your finished project will have against fingerprints, etc.

"Another important thing to remember is to make sure you're a Prepper not a Pooper, 'cause Lord knows, nobody likes a Pooper, especially a party pooper like Bob Williams down the street. Now that guy, he... well, that's a story for another day," said Mr. Ditmar as he drifted in and out of what seemed like a comedic trance.

"Here's six prep steps to remember—write 'em down. First: Before starting, you'll need to remove light switches, doorknobs, etc. and fix the damaged spots by patching and sanding all holes, cracks or nicks in the wall; then clean the walls. Second: Use painter's tape to mask the area to be painted. Third: Move any furniture out of the way and spread drop cloths on to the floor as well as anything that cannot easily be moved. Fourth: Paint the walls with primer. Fifth: After the primer dries, paint the walls, let them dry and then paint them again. Sixth: Remove the painter's tape, pick up the drop cloths, clean your brushes, etc. and put the furniture back in place.

"That's it and you're done. But remember," he continued, "primer is the key to unlocking a perfect finish! Hmm, that was pretty good. 'Unlocking' . . . 'key.' Hey, did you get that out there in the audience? 'Cause that was pretty good, heh, heh, heh. Feel free to use it!"

"Oh brother!" thought Sarah.

"Primer not only covers up colors and stains, it also adds a layer that allows the top coat of paint to better adhere, giving you more impressive results. Unless you're buying a primer and paint all in one, it's a good idea to prime first, especially when painting over new sheetrock or when drastically changing the wall color," instructed Mr. Ditmar.

"Now it's okay to cut in—I mean, after all, sometimes when you see a pretty lassie, you've just got to go over there and give her a little twirl. You know what I mean? Although, the misses didn't quite see it that way last time, but heck, that's a story for another day.

"Cutting in allows for smoother work when using rollers or larger brushes by first using a paintbrush to hit the areas they can't get to, like wall or ceiling corners, molding, etc. If you wait and try to do it after painting a larger area, it will create uneven lines. So remember, cut in first, before somebody else cuts in front of you! Heh, heh, heh, heh. Well, that's all I got! Go out and make me proud."

It wasn't clear if the Decorating Club members were just overly anxious to make him proud or they were just in a huge hurry to start painting. Either way, they quickly fled the home of one Mr. Eli Ditmar and headed directly to the nearest paint store. After picking up the needed materials, they raced back and began prepping the room.

Design Element—Fabric

Jackie volunteered to head up the sewing committee and began locating the fabric based on one of Tricia's swatches. Luckily, each girl on the committee owned a sewing machine and offered to bring it to Jackie's workroom. After setting up, they got to work busily making four sets of lined panel curtains out of a pretty pink taffeta material. Jackie also picked up a pink-and-white checked fabric that she used to make a chair pad for Tricia's newly updated desk.

Design Element—Accessories

Since the room was large enough to accommodate a reception area, the accessory committee helped Tricia plan the space.

They identified a roomy pink sofa with white fluffy accent pillows to go opposite the entrance door, as well as a contemporary coffee table to be positioned in front of the sofa and a studio chair covered in cheetah print to go alongside it.

A beautiful white chandelier was purchased to hang over the area, along with a tri-fold room divider to separate the area from the "office". Lastly, the room was further illuminated by a transitional lamp complete with cheetah shade.

They also found a framed and matted picture of a woman's head with motivational words written inside to hang on one of the walls and a pot of pink silk orchids, Tricia's favorite flower, to rest on the coffee table.

It seemed like Tricia's plan for 'How am I going to get there?' was really starting to take shape. The girls on the sewing committee finished sewing the panels and trimmed them with big pink pom-poms. Paul's old desk was given a major facelift and now sported a pink hue, accented with very feminine hardware.

Reshma told the group about an unemployed artist she knew from her church who specialized in painting signs. She suggested that he might be perfect for painting the quotes onto the wall. Tricia so loved the idea that tears streamed down her face.

However, Sarah had a sense that there was more going on behind Tricia's eyes than anyone knew, perhaps including Tricia.

CHAPTER 16

Take 2?

THE PHONE LINES LIT UP with the news of an emergency meeting. Everyone was to show up at Tricia's home the very next day, immediately after the bus left for school, and it was mandatory. Speculation and fear ran wild through the minds of Decorating Club members as they tried to weigh every possible reason for the meeting.

"I have to cancel our plans for my redesign," Tricia said softly. "I'm afraid I can't move forward with it, and I apologize for whatever upset this might bring."

"Oh no, I hope she's not going to tell us she went back to work again," thought Brittany.

"I wonder if she and Paul had another big fight and she's going to tell us they're getting a divorce," thought Tabatha.

"I hope it's not that her mother's sick again and she has to go take care of her," thought Reshma.

"Hmm, maybe she just changed her mind and fell in love with another color," thought Maggie.

"I can't imagine what could be up, she seemed so happy," thought Jackie.

"Well, Tricia, I'm sure the girls are also wondering. So will you please shed some light on why you can't move forward with the design for your office?" said Sarah.

"Yes, I can't move forward with the design because my story has changed. I just found out I'm pregnant!" screamed Tricia.

First, tears poured from the eyes of every member as they shared in Tricia's happy news. Next came all the questions one after another.

"How do you feel?"

"When are you due?"

"What did Paul say?"

"Well, at first I was thinking I must have caught some kind of stomach bug," she said with a smile as she started slowly answering. "I have roughly seven more months," she continued a little faster and louder, "and Paul doesn't know yet!" she screamed, and the girls squealed with delight.

"When are you going to tell him?" they asked.

"That's something I wanted to talk to all of you about. I'd like you guys to help me in telling him. I thought we could use the formula Sarah taught us—you know,

'Where am I?' 'Where am I going?' and 'How am I going to get there?' After all, that formula seems to be a key to success in all areas of life. So, I thought we could apply it in developing my plan for sharing the news with my husband.

"Paul is always telling me how much he appreciates creativity in advertising and in life. He says it can turn life's little moments into life's most memorable moments. In fact, he loves to repeat his favorite quote, 'Life is not measured by the number of breaths we take, but by the moments that take our breath away'. And I want this one to be a moment that takes his breath away, one that he will always remember," Tricia said, eyes glistening.

* * *

Now with the focus completely on Tricia's news, the team discussed the details and what was needed to complete her plan. "I need big sheets of white poster board as well as the name and number of the artist you mentioned from your church, Reshma. Also, I'll need lots of colorful balloons and for each of you to be here with your minivans right after the kids get on the bus this coming Friday morning."

When Friday morning finally arrived, the team was filled with excitement and anticipation to learn how Tricia planned to tell Paul her wonderful news.

"Follow me," said Tricia after they had loaded up all the minivans. And so the caravan took off, heading east toward Annapolis. "Okay, this is the where Paul works and where we're going to start," she told the women, who were eager to follow her instructions. Shortly after that, they packed up and headed back out onto Route 50 west retracing their steps back to Tricia's house. Along the way, they made several stops leaving another clue at each.

* * *

The five 'o clock bell rang, and Paul ran to his car. He was so intent on getting home early that he walked right past the first clue. Paul wanted to surprise Tricia and take her out for a romantic dinner, something he hadn't been able to do quite as frequently before due to Tricia's demanding work schedule and his own commitments to coaching. Now with Tricia home, Paul had been spending way less time on the field and more time with Tricia. As he jumped into the car, Paul noticed brightly colored balloons out of the corner of his eye. He smiled to

THE DECORATING CLUB

himself, surmising that some little boy or girl must be having a birthday party.

As he turned onto Route 50, he was faced with the usual wall of traffic. Determined not to let it spoil his mood, he searched for a relaxing radio station.

With his foot on the brake, Paul glanced to the right and noticed another one of the clues. There on the side of the road stuck into the ground was a neatly hand-painted sign with the words, "Congratulations, someone who takes this route to and from work is going to be a daddy!" Balloons of almost every color were tied to the stick, making it virtually impossible to miss.

"Oh boy," thought Paul, "there's one lucky guy out there!"

As he drove along, Paul found himself daydreaming and weighing the possibility of that ever happening to him. His concentration broke when he was greeted by yet another clue while taking the exit for Route 3 north. "Congratulations, someone who takes this exit is going to be a daddy!"

"Geez, another sign!"

Then a few moments later crossing Route 450 into Crofton, "Congratulations, someone who lives in this town is going to be a daddy!"

"Wow, I wonder if I know him."

A short while later, making a right onto Meadowbrook lane and into his community, Paul spied one more sign, "Congratulations, someone who lives on this street is going to be a daddy!"

"Okay, I definitely must know him. Maybe it's Matt up the block. They already have three, and Kathy has been looking a little puffy lately," he concluded.

But, there were no more signs. In fact, Paul didn't see any other clues along the entire one-mile trek to his home. That is until, as he pulled into the driveway, he was greeted by fifty or more brightly colored balloons and a huge sign over the doorway that read, "Congratulations, someone who lives in this house is going to be a daddy!"

"Oh Lord, it's ME!" Paul yelled.

Jerking the car to a stop, he jumped out and ran to the front door bursting through and then falling to his knees, where, as he stared at Tricia's beaming smile, he struggled to catch his breath.

* * *

Pink or Blue?

The men and women of the Decorating Club gathered once again in celebration. But this time instead of a cocktail party, it proved to be more of a working baby shower.

The women all arrived neatly dressed and carrying beautifully wrapped boxes trimmed with yellow and green bows. The men showed up in jeans carrying six-packs and an assortment of Cuban cigars.

After a flurry of handshakes and about a hundred slaps on the back, the men got to work dismantling what was once to be Tricia's office and now would be the nursery.

Paul shared his desire to surprise Tricia with a custom built-in wall-to-wall bookcase and asked his friends if they'd help.

"Absolutely!" exclaimed the men, and then off they ran to purchase wood and supplies.

"Tricia, do you know yet if you're having a boy or girl?" asked Reshma.

"No we don't and to be honest, Paul and I have decided we would rather be surprised," answered Tricia.

"Well, what about the room color? Would you like to paint over the pink, maybe something more neutral? We can ask the guys to help when they get back. I'm sure it won't take long," offered Sarah.

"No, I appreciate that, but it really doesn't matter. All that matters, whether boy or girl, is that it knows it's loved. Besides, if we do have a boy then we'll have a whole new excuse to have you guys back over to help in the future," Tricia said with a wink.

"Did you know that wasn't always the case—pink for girls and blue for boys?" said Jackie. "When I was attending FIT I learned that people years ago used to think that pink was a stronger color for boys since it was derived from red, and blue was considered daintier as well as a prettier color for girls. Yet opinions varied, and half the stores promoted pink, while the other stores believed blue was the better choice. It must have been a real fashion nightmare," laughed Jackie.

"Well, speaking of untraditional colors, quick, open my present before you change your mind about colors not mattering," urged Maggie.

Tricia quickly tore through the wrapping paper and opened the top of the box. Nestled just underneath the white tissue paper was a bold orange-and-purple hand-knit baby sweater.

"I received this wool years ago from my dear auntie in Ireland. She was a real firecracker, and you remind me of her. Anyway, she was the one who taught me how to knit. I've been hanging on to it until just the right occasion and well, I thought this was it. I hope you like it," said Maggie.

"Maggie, you're the best. I love it!" said Tricia.

"Open mine next," pleaded Reshma.

THE DECORATING CLUB

* * *

The women were so busy having a great time that they didn't even notice that the men had returned or what they were up to.

Several hours later, they asked the women to join them as they proudly unveiled the new nursery, complete with crib, changing table, antique rocking chair, and a beautiful wooden bookcase filled with a collection of cherished books from Tricia's childhood.

CHAPTER 17

The Gift Is in Giving

Project #4 - Brittany?

Where am I?

63 RIVA ROAD, Annapolis, MD

The address was the home of Brittany and David Cambridge and their three children, Elizabeth, Thomas and James.

The house rested on sixteen fully fenced and gated acres that overlooked the South River. It boasted over twenty-one thousand square feet and included seven bedrooms, ten bathrooms, a six-car garage and an egg-shaped swimming pool with adjoining pool house as well as a guesthouse, barn, and two woodsheds.

The main house had a formal ballroom with a stone fireplace, formal living room, formal dining room and gourmet kitchen with a breakfast room.

There was an entertainment room complete with bumper and regular pool tables and two-sided fireplaces, a movie theatre, a ballet room, a gym, a walk-in fireproof safe room, a library with a fireplace, a master suite with two bathrooms, an elevator and a lot more.

Sarah rang the bell and was greeted by Consuela, who humbly motioned for Sarah to follow her. As they walked down the very long hallway, Sarah couldn't help but notice the activity taking place in each one of the rooms they passed. Rugs were being rolled out, furniture was being moved and workers on ladders were busily hanging drapes.

Finally, she reached Brittany, who was in the middle of a conversation with a very tall, smartly dressed man in a dark blue two-button wool suit.

"Oh, hello, Sarah, let me introduce you to Robert. He's my lead designer," she said in a matter-of-fact kind of way.

"It's nice to meet you," said Sarah, who was captivated by Robert's shoulder-length blond hair and beautiful looks.

"Thank you, sweetie, you too," he said before walking away.

"Sweetie? Who is this guy?" thought Sarah. "And why does Brittany have all these design people here, especially today?"

Within fifteen minutes, the rest of the Decorating Club members arrived and the Brittany House Tour commenced. The girls marveled as they peeked into the most magnificent rooms many had ever seen. There were ornate chandeliers, oil paintings under spotlights, impressive vases; grand pianos and what seemed like enough furniture to fill one hundred typical homes. The tour, by way of elevator, took just over two hours. The women stopped at every doorway to look into each ostentatious room as Brittany provided color and commentary before moving on to the next.

"Brittany, why exactly are we here? Your home looks like a show house, and there doesn't appear to be one room that needs a redesign. Besides, it's clear that you have a team of interior designers already on staff," said Sarah in a very confused tone.

"Okay, that's true, but there is one room where I'd like everyone's help. It's my husband David's library. Sarah, I was moved by your philosophy that a house should tell the story of the people who live there, and I want your help creating a story for David," said Brittany.

"I don't understand," Sarah replied with a puzzled look. "Brittany, surely you know your husband better than any of us."

"Well, yes, but let me explain a little. You see, I like to entertain, and we do it quite regularly. Whenever we have company I usually take the women around to see the house, and then we go into the grand ballroom. The men join my husband in his library, where they sit and have cocktails before dinner. I need that room to have more personality, so the men are captivated enough to stay there longer rather than rushing out to disturb us," she said pointedly.

"Well if that's the case, you need to tell me and the rest of the members more about David; we've only had a very limited exposure to him. You need to fill in the blanks like what he does for a living and how he likes to enjoy his time off; what his hobbies are; and any other things he's interested in," pressed Sarah as she tried to guide the conversation.

"What's there to tell, he's very boring. All he does is fly all over the world working. He's an executive for a multinational financial services company and heads up their credit card division. There's not much else to tell you," said Brittany in an impatient tone.

"I'm afraid you'll have to give us more than that, or we're not going to be able to help you," said Sarah.

"Okay, let me think. Oh yes, I remember something that might be helpful. There is a box that David keeps upstairs in his closet. It's filled to overflowing with items he received from dignitaries and business executives from various countries. They are what he refers to as 'deal toys.' I haven't seen any of them, but he said they were treasures given to him by very important people. I can have Consuela take you up there to look through it while I finish up with Robert," said Brittany.

* * *

SUSAN M. MEYERS

* * *

A Home

A home is more than a mixture of florals and stripes
A home is a reflection of our days and our nights
A creative expression of interests and thoughts
A house is a home when filled with comfort and warmth.

* * *

Sarah and the rest of the team followed Consuela down the hall to the small elevator.

"Hey, Tricia, why don't you just take the ride with Consuela and we'll all meet you upstairs outside the master suite?" said Sarah.

As they entered the room, Consuela, who didn't speak very much English, pointed to a double set of oak doors and said, "Senor David's armario." The girls proceeded through the doorway and into a room that was larger than almost any room in their homes.

"Oh my gosh, this looks like the inside of Barney's. Look at all these suits and shirts!" exclaimed Jackie.

"Yes, and so organized with them all in color groupings and then stripes and checks. Ooh, my Anil would go crazy if he saw this." Reshma giggled.

"Wow, look at this," said Maggie as she pointed to a wooden case filled with thirty different Mont Blanc pens. "One for every day of the month," she said as she raised her hand then pointed her pinky up into the air.

Way deep in the back of the closet was a large brown cardboard box with the word Gifts on it.

"This must be it," said Sarah as she blew the dust off the top of the box.

Almost as though directed, the girls all sat down on the carpet in a circle surrounding Sarah, as if they were back in kindergarten awaiting "story time."

The first thing Sarah pulled out was a small statue of Arabian horses with a personalized note from the Tunisian ambassador. The next was an oil painting of the original bust of Tsar Alexander I of Russia. There also was a prayer flag from the Tiger's Nest Monastery that was encased in a beautiful, ornate glass frame. There were bottles of wine from French dignitaries, a white tulip vase from the prime minister of the Netherlands, black leather riding boots from the Australian prime minister, and a collection of many other items, including paintings, miniature sculptures, gem-encrusted vases, rare books, traditional clothing, photo portraits from what appeared to be heads of state and monarchs and a beautiful white gold men's wristwatch on a leather band, that had been gifted to David by the Saudi king.

"Oh my gosh," screamed Tricia, "she's crazy not to have seen any of this!"

They all agreed, and Sarah struggled to herself to see how a couple that apparently had so much could seem to have so little. It was clear to her that despite all they had, the couple lived separate lives.

Where am I going?

David's library was indicative of an old English parlor or drawing room. It included well-worn leather club chairs, dark wood paneling and built-in bookshelves. It also had an antique billiards table, oriental rugs, a well-stocked wooden circular bar with padded stools, a collection of antique maps and an enormous fireplace all adding to the exquisite blend of old and new.

"This certainly isn't going to be like the rest of our redesigns," thought Sarah.

The room was already serving its intended purpose. So, the challenge for the Decorating Club would be to enhance and re-energize the feel of the room to have it reflect David's personality and experiences.

Sarah felt that could be achieved by incorporating a strategic selection of items from among the many interesting gifts and artifacts he had accumulated as he traveled the globe, and could be done in a subtle, artful and thought-provoking way.

"But that's just a piece of David's story," Sarah thought. "To be complete it needs to include his personal story as well, and that means his family and his relationship with Brittany!"

After returning downstairs, Sarah asked Brittany, "Do you and David have any special pictures of the two of you together? Or perhaps a cherished family photo of the two of you with the kids that we could display in the room?"

"No, not really," Brittany quietly responded, "We haven't had any pictures of us taken in a long time.

David's never around and the ones we do have of our children are very outdated."

"What about something romantic like a love poem or notes to each other?" asked Jackie.

"Hmm, if you asked me that question when we were back in college, I'd be able to say yes. David was very romantic then and was always writing me notes and poems," Brittany responded, smiling as she thought of days gone by.

"Unfortunately, since then, as the saying goes, 'life happened' and David's become more and more preoccupied with his career and less focused on romantic gestures. But there is one thing," Brittany started, and then suddenly went quiet for a moment. "I gave David a note years ago that I know he saved. Maybe we can somehow include it," she said in a way that seemed like she was softening.

Then, excusing herself, Brittany went upstairs to the second master bathroom, the one designated for David. Tucked away in one of his drawers was the note Brittany had referred to, and she smiled as she reread her words written to David so many years ago.

"Well it's true, I still would!" she said as tears began to stream down her face.

Brittany had written the note to David when he was up for a promotion with his company. At the time, the company was exploring the possibility of transferring him to their office in Zimbabwe, and he was fearful that Brittany wouldn't want to go. Instead, Brittany presented him with a gift of limited edition Trafalgar braces, reminiscent of a safari expedition, and a simple note that said, "I'll follow you anywhere!"

How am I going to get there?

On the way back to her friends struggling to focus on the "redesign" of David's library, Brittany couldn't help but dwell upon the past and how the tender, romantic relationship she and David once shared had seemingly dried up. Nowadays, it seemed as though David was traveling even more than ever, and at times Brittany was convinced it was just a convenient excuse for him not to be at home. Even more troubling was that their children were quickly growing up and doing so without really knowing their father.

"I don't even know him anymore," thought Brittany, "and I'm just as much to blame. I've consumed myself with decorating this oversized, overstuffed house instead of addressing what's most important. This isn't a home; it's just a big, stuffy shell. "

Then Brittany was suddenly reminded of what her father used to tell her whenever she felt trapped by some decision or circumstance. "If you paint yourself into a corner, watching the paint dry is seldom the best solution."

"Thanks, Dad, you're right. This has to stop, and I'm going to change things right now!"

Then, upon returning to the girls, Brittany proclaimed, "Ladies, it's time to shake things up!" startling them a bit as they wondered what exactly Brittany had in mind.

"What do you wish to do, and how can we help?" asked Reshma.

"Yes, how can we help?" added Tricia.

"Well, first things first, I still want to move forward with our plan to create a space that represents David and his accomplishments, both career and personal. I want the room filled with all the things that make him who he is." After taking a deep breath, Brittany continued, "And then I plan to release all the workers and have you help me dismantle and simplify the existing decorating themes of this house, room by room. Afterwards, once David, the children and I have spent time working on our own story, we can go back and refill each room as a family to ensure that it represents who we are and why," said Brittany in a very strong and positive tone.

Somewhat stunned by Brittany's announcement, the women stood quietly for a few moments.

Then Tabatha spoke up. "That sounds very exciting, Brittany, but what are you going to tell David, not to mention Robert and all the workers?"

"Oh that's easy. I simply plan to tell them I changed my mind," Brittany said with a smile.

The girls all laughed and celebrated her courageous decision. They also agreed to assist, so the dismantling began immediately. Brittany's army of decorators and artisans were dismissed; black bags were filled, donation places were called and eBay was now flooded with new inventory.

The once pompous, institutional feel of David's library was replaced with a casual man-cave type atmosphere that both shared his interests and accomplishments with its visitors as well as his passions and loves. Now mixed in right alongside Russian tea sets and pictures of monarchs were World's Greatest Dad mugs and hand-painted pictures of hearts.

The massive fireplace that once was the primary focal point of the room now played second fiddle to a simple frame that was displayed atop its mantel containing a special, handwritten, and worn note that read:

"I'll follow you anywhere!"

* * *

The Invite

Please join David and me as we host the next Decorating Club party.

This surely will stand out from all the rest, for our redesign has become more of an undress.

We're still happy to walk you around from floor to floor, but keep in mind, the elevator's no longer part of the tour.

Our house, once a museum filled with crystals, tassels, fine linens and lace, is now empty except for humility, laughter, love and the presence of grace.

No need for pity, or to view our lack of possessions as a void, for we've turned our stuffy one into a "party house" on steroids

We are looking forward to seeing you on Friday night. Get ready to kick up your heels and join in our delight.

  Fondly,

  Brittany and David

THE DECORATING CLUB

"Yes, it is a small world after all!"

Each couple was handed a map and a passport as they entered the front door, then directed to await further instruction.

"Wow, this is really different—are we going on some sort of trip?" asked Paul.

"Hey, David, is the jet parked and fueled out in the back? Do you need me to run home and jump into my uniform?" taunted Mark.

"Hey, buddy, if I knew we were going on a trip I would have brought you a nice bottle of Scotch instead of this cheap bottle of red," teased Eric as he handed the bottle of wine to David.

"Nope, sorry, guys, your feet aren't going to leave the ground tonight, unless of course you drink too much," countered David.

Just then, Brittany joined up with the group in the foyer. "Hi, everyone thanks for coming to our Decorating Club Party. I know this project was a bit different, and as I explained we aren't ready for our redesign yet, but David and I felt it important to have all of you guys over now anyway and . . ."

"We came up with what we think is going to be a fun, tasty and informative agenda for the evening," David jumped in.

"That's right," Brittany continued. "The whole idea came to us after I shared your 3D strategy with David, Sarah. We both love the idea of turning flat boring spaces into lively rooms filled with meaningful atmosphere."

"So we've transformed all of our unoccupied rooms into travel destinations for tonight. As you walk around you'll be able to see some of the colors and textures used to decorate in other parts of the world, as well as sample their food, hear their music and learn a bit about their customs. We urge you to visit as many as you can.

"Hey, do you have a room representing Mexico by any chance?" inquired Paul.

"Yes we do. Why, Pablo, do you have some sort of special interest in Mexico?" David jokingly fired back.

"Well, yes, as a matter of fact I think there's probably a margarita there with my name on it," Paul replied as he busted out laughing.

"Okay, let the journey begin!" declared David.

Besides Mexico, the room representing Germany also ended up being a huge favorite among the male members of the Decorating Club. There they sampled German beer and pretzels and enjoyed a variety of bratwurst and sausage while listening to Oom-pah music.

The most exciting part of the evening, though, came several hours later, or better put, two too many beer steins later—when Paul, moved by the music, decided to teach the rest of his pals the German slap-fighting dance.

While the tradition originated as a courtship dance, it quickly became obvious that each of the men were more interested in trying to outdo the others than impress their ladies. They delighted in the no-holds-barred slap-fighting part of the activity and flew through the air with powerful leaps.

The evening closed with Sarah and Tommy heading to the emergency room as a result of an overly exuberant slap that came more in the form of a punch.

CHAPTER 18

Navigating Change

Project #5 - Tabatha and Eric

DIFFERENT, NOT BAD or good different, just different. Tabatha and Eric are just those kind of people. Both are strong and independent souls who share a rather unique love and passion for each other. Despite having met and married over thirty-four years ago, they continue to project a newlywed aura to this day.

Tabatha loves working for herself and over the years has had one creative business after another. Eric on the other hand is analytic by nature, known for his forward thinking and a natural-born leader. While perceived by some as a power couple, they often laughed at the suggestion and actually are more comfortable with a

"Renaissance" label for they feel that better reflects their desire to continually learn, explore their talents and work to improve their lives and the lives of those around them—especially the lives of their twin grandsons Taylor and Ryan.

Yet while outsiders may see nothing but bliss, Tabatha and Eric have had their share of challenges—with the greatest being the loss of their only child.

Eric's day job is VP of sales for CPG, a well-known, publicly traded consumer packaged goods firm. He oversees the branding, marketing and promotion of a snack line that targets health-conscious consumers. Although the office he works out of is in Washington, DC, Eric travels about 40 percent of the time, delivering sales presentations to prospective clients and major accounts of CPG. He has worked for the company for many years, is well liked and excels at his position. However, Eric has started wondering what life's next chapter has in store for him.

It isn't that he dislikes his job or the people where he works. He believes there's more for him to do with his life, but just what is not clear to him. He also has noticed many of his friends are retiring, and Eric is beginning to reflect on what that would look like for him and Tab.

On the other hand, Tabatha feels that Eric won't find the answer by just turning in his "key card." She knows that her husband has always been a strong, vital man who never gives in to a challenge. Tabatha views both this time-period and Eric's mindset as just the next trial for him to attack and conquer. He has too much to offer to just unplug from life.

A few years back, Tabatha and Eric decided to pursue and ultimately enjoy a plant-based diet. It's a lifestyle that was introduced to them because of what Eric had learned from reading The China Study by T. Colin Campbell, PhD, and Thomas M. Campbell II, MD. He was given the book while onboard a plane returning home from a business trip. Sitting next to Eric was an exuberant young woman who had just attended a cooking class taught by a renowned vegan chef. She gushed about the program and declared to Eric, "The wave of the future is veganism, and you should jump on the surfboard." Encouraging him to learn more about it and seeing that Eric showed an interest, she graciously offered him her copy of the book she got at the class. Eric never forgot about their encounter, the young woman's gesture and her prophecy about the future. In fact, since that time he often daydreams about one day creating and marketing his own brand of vegan snack bars.

Initially, Tabatha was not at all happy about giving up meat, poultry, fish, eggs and dairy. Confused, angry and frustrated, she asked, "What do we now say we are when friends and relatives ask? Should I say we're vegetarians or vegans or should I just say we're aliens?"

Eric smiled and said, "I don't care what people call me, and if they ask I'll tell them I'm a Tabatha."

"What's that supposed to mean?" she demanded.

In a calm positive tone, Eric responded, "It's simple, honey. It means that I have decided to eat a plant-based diet so I can stay healthy and be around for as long as I can for my beautiful wife, Tabatha."

After a moment, smiling somewhat begrudgingly, Tabatha softly declared. "Okay, you got me, but I'm not going to cook boring, bland and tasteless food! Instead, you're going to have to send me to one of those gourmet vegan-cooking classes you told me about!".

"Great honey, it's a deal," said Eric.

Where am I?

Eric and Tabatha live in Davidsonville, Maryland; approximately fifteen minutes away from most of the other girls who, except for Brittany, all resided in Crofton.

They had recently built a barn on a portion of their property. With the twins getting older, they felt it was the perfect answer to their growing need for extra space and thought it would also provide an escape for some "alone time." Their plan was for Eric to relocate all of his workout equipment out of his "boiler room" gym in their basement and into the "fitness area" located in the barn. Another section of the barn would serve as a creative art studio for Tabatha to comfortably explore her varied interests while "looking to spot an un-fulfilled need in the marketplace" and then strive to fulfill it.

As it turned out, the barn was more than big enough to accommodate both activities and still left a large common area available. While neither Tabatha nor Eric were quite sure of how to use the space, they were confident that with the help of the Decorating Club they would figure it out.

* * *

"This is adorable," commented Maggie as she walked up to the barn, newly painted red and trimmed in white.

"And I just love the cute window boxes with all the pretty flowers," said Tricia.

"Thanks, guys. Come on in and I'll show you around," Tabatha proudly replied.

"Did you say round or around?" Sarah jokingly asked.

"Yeah, this is the first round barn I've ever seen. I didn't know they could be round," said Jackie.

"Um, actually, George Washington owned one, and I think he even may have invented it," volunteered Reshma.

"How did you know that, Reshma?" asked Tricia.

"Well, hmmmh, I'm not really sure, but I think I remember reading it when I was studying to become an American citizen," she replied.

"Well, I never heard of a round barn either. That is, until we decided to build one. But apparently, the circular form has a greater volume-to-surface ratio than the more traditional rectangular or square forms. I don't fully understand exactly what that means, but Eric was excited about it." Tabatha laughed.

"Well since I majored in biology maybe I can help. Perhaps it would be easier to explain by analogy. For example, if you think of a glass of water. The volume is the area in the glass that the water takes up. By contrast, the bottom of the glass, the part that leaves the nasty circle on your freshly polished coffee table—" Tricia grinned "—is the surface area of the glass. In conclusion, my example demonstrates that the surface area of the glass is smaller than its volume, just like Tabatha's round barn, and that completes my 411 on volume."

"Well that makes sense. Thanks, Tricia. With less surface area, we were able to use fewer building materials, and that saved us a lot on the cost to build it.

Plus, it's supposed to offer greater structural stability than rectangular barns, so I don't have to worry as much about wolves showing up to huff and puff and blow our barn down," Tabatha added with a smile.

"We really like the open feel of the space. As you can see, over there are Eric's weights, and on this side is where I have my art supplies. But we are struggling to figure out what to do with the space in the middle and are hopeful that you guys can help us," Tabatha explained while pointing out the different areas.

"Why didn't you guys put up any interior walls and doors to separate the areas?" asked Brittany.

"Well, shortly after Eric and I met and fell in love, he explained that we must be careful to never build up walls between us. He meant it figuratively, of course, but literally, he said he would never get tired of seeing my face. I know that sounds corny, but what can I say, I feel the same way about him," said Tabatha, beginning to blush.

"I think that's adorable and very sweet. You don't see many people love each other the way you guys do, especially after how long you've been together. Oh yeah, by the way, how did you guys meet anyway?" questioned Sarah.

"Oh, that's a long story, Sarah. I don't want to bore you guys," said Tabatha.

"You're not going to bore us," said Brittany.

"Yes, tell us," said Reshma.

"Okay, but first let's all go inside and get a cup of coffee," said Tabatha.

"Hmm, that's one thing we definitely could use in this barn. If I had a kitchen I wouldn't have to run back and forth into the house," Tabatha thought as she took one more look at the space before shutting the barn door behind her.

Once inside and before sitting down, each of the girls filled their cups and grabbed what appeared to be a freshly baked health bar from the platter. "Okay, are you sure you want to hear our story?" asked Tabatha.

"Yes!" said the members as they each nodded.

"Well, it was 1985 and I decided that I needed a vacation. At the time, I owned a vinyl repair company and could pretty much set my own work schedule. As a result, I had the opportunity to travel as often as I wanted, or I should say as often as I could afford. It was a great little business, and back then, vinyl was everywhere, including in most homes and in almost every business establishment. I would work very hard repairing as much ripped and torn vinyl as it took to buy a round-trip ticket and then hop on a plane for a vacation. Once I returned, I'd do it all over again, working until I had enough money to buy my next ticket. Needless to say, I did and do love to travel. Anyway, my best friend and travel companion at the time was Kathy Anderson. We were planning our next trip, and it was going to be an island vacation; that is, until Darlene, Kathy's friend, decided to join us.

"The plans quickly changed from visions of sun, sand, and surf to backpacks, hiking boots and blisters. Although I initially moved forward with the plans my heart wasn't in it, it wasn't really me. Then one day, I heard a radio commercial for an all-inclusive vacation. I previously had been on a similar trip and loved the fact that everything was included in the price. As I listened, a few things caught my attention: tropical paradise, no extra fee to travel solo and unlimited waterskiing, so I followed my instincts and said sign me up!

"Without hesitation I went right down to the travel agency and booked myself on the next chartered trip. The fact that it was to Haiti and I would need to take malaria pills didn't really faze me at the time. Nor did I realize that Haiti was among the poorest nations in the Western Hemisphere, if not the world. That coupled with its political unrest, a struggling economy and being rumored to be a possible birthplace of AIDS caused my mom to be less than excited about the trip.

"But, in my mind, it was just a great deal for another adventure in a warm tropical destination that offered as much waterskiing as I wanted. Besides, I didn't know anyone who had ever been to Haiti before, and I thought that sounded kind of cool.

"A guy friend of mine dropped me off at the airport and gave me a farewell kiss, and off I went to board my direct flight to Port-au-Prince, Haiti. Once all the passengers were on board, the mood quickly switched to full party mode. Music and singing echoed loudly throughout the cabin, drinks flowed nonstop and buzzed passengers instantly turned from strangers into friends right before my eyes.

"Seated next to me were two girls from Austin. They were very excited about the trip and spoke nonstop about the prospects for a Vegas-like vacation—you know, 'What happens in Haiti, stays in Haiti.' Yet shortly after we landed the entire mood took a 180."

"Oh no, what happened?"

"Shhhh, Reshma! Let her continue," scolded Tricia.

"Well I remember thinking, 'I'm not in Kansas anymore.' It actually was a bit scary. The Port-au-Prince airport was very small, hot and seemed to have lots of security guards. It was nothing at all like Dallas-Fort Worth, or any other airport I had ever seen. After we finished picking up our luggage, the tour people loaded us in small groups onto old, brightly painted 'tap-tap' buses, and we headed off through the countryside on what was, for me, the most depressing journey imaginable."

"Tap-tap busses?" quizzed Tricia.

"Yes, Tricia, that's what they call the little independently owned trolley-like busses that make up most of the Haitian transportation system. If I recall correctly, the ride to our destination took about an hour, but it seemed more like forever. It was so sad, and I remember seeing people living right there on the side of the road. Their shelters appeared to consist of large banana leaves secured together by mud. Then, as we finally reached the resort, it was like an armed camp. It even had a guard station in front.

"Although the club itself was beautiful, we were all warned not to leave the property. It was like a magical fairy tale inside the gates, but the outside reflected nothing but poverty and depression. I found it hard not to feel guilty being there on vacation while the people outside appeared to be barely surviving." Tabatha sighed.

"Well, back to my story, two days later, I ran into the girls from the plane and sat down with them next to the pool. After about an hour they started to complain about how it seemed that while there were like two thousand people currently at the resort, not one of them was a cute guy. Just then, I happened to look up from my book and said, 'That guy's kinda cute.' Little did I know that the guy splashing around diving for the volleyball, and I later learned, doing his best to get my attention, would soon become the man I'd say 'I do' to.

"Eric and I met the following day, and he later told me that he'd actually seen me in the airport, when my friend dropped me off—adding that he noticed him give me a kiss. But, since Eric hadn't seen him at the resort for the past two days, he decided to look for an opportunity to talk to me.

"As we took a walk down the beach, he asked me if I knew how to sail. Since the answer was no, Eric offered to teach me, and off we went in a cute little sailboat. We had a wonderful time getting to know each other and apparently had been sailing for quite a while. In the meantime, the club staff were having a meeting on the top floor of the main building. Then, we later learned, all of a sudden someone noticed far off in the distance the resort logo on the sail of our boat. They were shocked at the possibility and not quite sure what to do.

"Finally, one brave young man took action, and the next thing we knew, a boat was approaching us at record speed. Upon reaching us he began screaming and yelling in several different languages, ordering us to get into the bottom of his boat and to keep our heads down. Then he tied our little sailboat to the stern of his speedboat and we took off back to shore like a rocket. I wondered what the problem was; the boats were included as one of the activities, and besides, I hadn't sunk it. Overall, I thought I had done a really good job for my first lesson. 'Don't you realize that you almost sailed into Cuban waters that are patrolled by gunboats, not to mention you were sailing in shark-infested waters?' he screamed at us," said Tabatha.

"Oh my goodness, you are so lucky to be alive," chimed in Jackie.

"I know," continued Tabatha, "but wait, remember the almost two thousand people I mentioned also being at the club? Well when we finally arrived back, it looked like the entire group was standing there on the shore. As we exited the boat, they started clapping for our safe return and especially for the bravery of the guy who rescued us. I was so embarrassed." Tabatha sighed at the girls' laughter.

"We spent the rest of the vacation much more mildly, happily learning all about each other, while both secretly wondering what was happening. Then on the last day of our trip, I remember looking up into the sky as we walked out to the plane and saying, 'I don't want to leave.' Eric simply took my hand in his as we boarded, looked into my eyes, and said, 'Come on, it's time to go and start our life together,' and that's exactly what happened," Tabatha said smiling as she wiped her eyes.

"That is so beautiful. Thank you so much for sharing your story with us," said Sarah.

"Yes, that was amazing, yet so unbelievably sad for all the people of Haiti. Are things still as bad?" asked Maggie.

"Unfortunately, it seems as if the poor people living there regularly have a bullseye on their backs; yet it's amazing how resilient they are."

"Geez, that's truly a shame, but also seems to be an amazing example of strength and fortitude," observed Tricia.

"I agree," said Brittany. "Oh, but you never told us, why do they call them tap-tap busses?"

"Well, Brittany, the name tap-tap translates to 'quick-quick', but ironically the busses don't start moving until they are completely loaded with passengers—and then only along very limited, specific routes. Nonetheless, they serve to brighten the otherwise dreary, unrepaired streets of Port-au-Prince. Each is essentially a moving canvas—displaying the colorful work of the local artists and reflecting the thoughts and interests of the Haitian people. It's also interesting how some of the busses include portraits of American and international sports players and celebrities as part of the same canvas. It's almost as if they're saying, 'We may not have much, but we too have our dreams.'"

Where am I going?

Later that day, Tabatha had a chance to reflect on her time spent with the other members.

Although she still had no answer to the direction or use for the extra space in the barn, Tabatha enjoyed reminiscing about how she and Eric met. A smile formed as she thought about how crazy in love they were right from the start. "Just a couple of dumb kids; we were so lucky to have made it out of there without incident," she thought. Then her mind drifted to the tap-tap busses. "Those poor people. It's not as easy for them to leave; I just don't know how they do it. Every day they face many difficult challenges, and yet they seem to never give in to any of them."

Tabatha zeroed in on the symbolism. "We're so privileged to live in a land that fosters dreams. We have the opportunity to drive our own bus and choose our own destinations as we take charge of our own lives. Yet the people of Haiti have to rely on overcrowded buses as their source of transportation. Unable to come and go when or where they please. We, on the other hand, are so blessed. We are able to change our route anytime we wish and even add new stops along the way."

That prompted Tabatha to think about Eric and life's next chapter for the two of them.

How am I going to get there?

"Hey Tab, your men are back, where are you woman?"

Tabatha was in the barn when she saw Eric pull into the driveway and ran out to meet him, Ryan and Taylor.

"Here's my guys! I'm so glad your back, I missed you so much, a week was way too long," she said as she hugged her two grandsons.

"Did you have fun?"

"Yeah it was great! We slept on the ground and built a campfire and had s'mores and it was really cool," said Taylor.

"Yeah and we even saw a bear!" added Ryan.

"A bear??!!!" questioned Tabatha.

"Umm, yeaaah, we'll talk about that later. Boys why don't you go unpack now and take a nice long shower," insisted Eric.

"Okay," they both said as they ran toward the house.

"Now what is this about a bear?" questioned Tabatha.

"Eh, it was just a little one Tab not a big deal, don't worry we were completely safe. Sooo did you miss me?" he asked as he leaned in and wrapped his arms around Tabatha.

"Of course I missed you but I'm so glad you had this time alone with the boys. We both know how short life is and how we need to make every moment count – which reminds me I have something I want to talk to you about."

"Oh ok, go ahead I'm all ears."

Well, I've been thinking about incorporating a few new destinations to our journey."

"Alright, I just came home though so can I take a quick shower first?" Eric replied in a teasing manner.

"I didn't mean it like that silly"

Okay, babe, then...where would you like us to go?"

"Well, I'd like to turn the open space in our barn into a professional kitchen where we will produce and market the delicious blueberry health bars you've created! Based upon what I've already begun to research, we have more than enough space for the oven, refrigerator and other necessary equipment it would require," she said before continuing.

"This is something you've been talking about doing for forever, and I think now is the perfect time to start. Once it's all set up, I can bake several batches of bars each day while you're at work, and you can develop our marketing and distribution strategy in your spare time. On the weekends we'll join forces, and before you know it, we'll be so busy and successful that you'll have to quit your job so you can manage our business full time," she said without coming up for air.

Eric tilted his head slightly so that his glasses slid to the center of his nose. Then he looked Tabatha squarely in the eyes and asked, "And why do I want to do that?"

With a devilish smile, Tabatha quickly responded, "Because you're a Tabatha, and you want to stay healthy for me, physically and mentally. Besides, what is it that you're always telling me about turning a tanker?"

Eric smiled and said, "You can't turn a tanker quickly, so when you know that you'll need to change course, you have to start early."

"That's right! Sooo, I've started to 'turn our tanker.' I've even begun to consider packaging ideas."

"Wow Tab, I've only been gone a week; you do work quickly!" joked Eric.

Tabatha then handed Eric a picture she had drawn envisioning how their label might look. "It's only a rough sketch but what do you think?"

"Wow, that's amazing, I love every bit of it" Eric replied. "Especially the name, Tab Bar!" Then he moved in to warmly hug Tabatha and softly kiss her on the lips.

* * *

In lieu of a cocktail party, and in recognition of the Decorating Club's spirit of neighbors helping neighbors, the couple decided to host a barn-raising celebration.

They came up with the idea based upon a tradition of the Amish, a society grounded in the Christian belief of mutual aid. The barn raising would combine both the effort and reward in the same event.

At 7:00 a.m., the members and their husbands began to show up on the property. The women brought all kinds of food, and the men brought all kinds of tools. While the men were busily at work assembling what would soon be the home of the new Tab Bar, the women began cooking so they could provide the men with the needed fuel for the day.

Finally, at the six o'clock hour, the professional barn kitchen was built, in place and christened with a bottle of Dom Pérignon champagne.

CHAPTER 19

Thankful Thursday

"MOM... MOM... MOM... Mom... Mom!" shouted Sarah's youngest daughter as she ran up the steps to Sarah and Tommy's bedroom.

"What is it, Katie?" yelled Sarah as she came out to meet her.

"I'm thankful, I'm thankful, I'm thankful. I'm so very thankful," declared Katie.

"Okay, Katie, that's wonderful, but calm down and tell me what you're thankful for."

"Mister Spotty, Mom... Mister Spotty... I taught him and it finally worked!" she screamed.

"What worked, Katie? Tell me what you're talking about," she begged.

"Okay, remember how I have Meghan's Party on Saturday and we're supposed to bring our talented pet?" she said.

"Um, yes, alright, oh . . . yes, yes, I remember," said Sarah.

"Well, Maddie won't lend me Cottontail. I really wanted to bring her 'cause you know how she does that cool pooping trick. Well anyway, Collin said I couldn't bring Sadie either because she belonged to the whole family and didn't belong to just me, so I've been teaching Mister Spotty tricks. Today my teacher, Ms. Kravitz, said we have to tell the class what we're thankful for every Thursday from now on starting tomorrow, and now I know exactly what I'm going to say," she said breathlessly.

"Oh, well, that's great, honey. I'm glad, but what trick did you teach Mr. Spotty?" Sarah asked.

"I taught him to play dead, and he's doing it really good. I just saw him in his fish bowl floating on top of the water. I'm so excited, Mom. Now I have something really cool to share with my class about what I'm thankful for," she exclaimed as she ran back down the stairs.

"Ooooh, I don't have the heart to tell her," Sarah thought to herself, and then smiled. "I think this is going to have to be a Daddy job."

"Hmm, but I do love Miss Kravitz's idea; it's so nice to see her remind the kids to focus on all the things they have to be grateful for instead of just taking things for granted. Wow that just gave me an idea!"

THE DECORATING CLUB

* * *

"Good afternoon, you've reached Reynolds Tavern in Annapolis. How may I help you?" said the soft-spoken voice.

"Yes, hi, I'd like to make a reservation for afternoon tea at around one o'clock tomorrow–oh, and there will be seven of us," said Sarah.

* * *

"Wow, this place is so quaint and charming. It looks like it's been here forever," said Reshma.

"Actually, it has. Reynold's Tavern is the oldest tavern in Annapolis and one of the oldest in the United States. On top of that, their afternoon tea is to die for!" exclaimed Sarah.

"Well I for one am happy to be out of my painting clothes today and be here to enjoy it with all of you guys," remarked Tabatha.

"Yeah, this was a great idea, Sarah, but are we celebrating anything special? It's not your birthday, is it?" asked Brittany.

"Nope, no cake and candle for me today. I was just reminded of how much I have to be grateful for. Meeting all of you has changed my life, and I thought it would be cool to create a special memory with you guys. I'd like to dub today Thankful Thursday, and maybe we can all share some of the things we're thankful for—sort of like Thanksgiving," said Sarah.

"I think that's nice, Sarah. Would you mind if I went first?" asked Tricia.

"Sure, Tricia, go ahead," said Sarah.

"Well I believe that Maggie really unlocked the door to gratitude for me," said Tricia.

"I did? How did I do that?" asked Maggie.

"Remember when you shared how you were able to make the connection between a regular diet and a mental diet, well that really helped me change my thinking. Since then, I strive always to remain focused on the good in my life, and that has been very helpful in preventing fear from sabotaging me. Trust me, there are some weeks that are filled with nothing but Mondays, you know when I've had to start all over again. But for the most part I've been able to replace my fear with thankfulness," said Tricia.

"That's awesome, Tricia, and to be honest I owe you thanks too," said Sarah.

"Me? I think you've got that backward, Sarah!" declared Tricia.

"No, I don't. When we were working on your project, you said, 'I intend to take charge and regain my life' and you did, and you've inspired me to start doing the same!

Do any of you guys play tennis? I want to start playing again, and I need a practice buddy," admitted Sarah.

"I'll play with you, Sarah. I have a weekly court time on Thursday nights over at the place on Route 3," said Brittany.

"Excellent!" Sarah exclaimed while giving a thumbs up.

"Ok, my contribution might pale in comparison, but it's a true story, only it didn't happen to me. It's so funny, though, and I've been dying to tell you guys, and I can't keep it in any longer," said Tabatha.

"Tell us, tell us!" demanded the members.

"Okay, so here goes. My sister Heather, who lives in Connecticut, told me that a couple of weeks ago she got tagged for jury duty but didn't think she'd actually have to serve. So she went to court on the morning she was scheduled to report, and—"

"Wait a minute, why was Heather so sure she wasn't going to serve?" interrupted Jackie.

"Oh yeah, sorry. Heather told me she heard from a friend that the judge typically would ask you if you have family members who are attorneys or work in law enforcement or if there was another reason that might influence your decision on the case. Since my brother-in-law and a number of his family members work in those types of professions, Heather thought for sure they'd send her home right away.

"But instead they called her name and had her report to one of the judge's chambers with a whole big group of other potential jurors," said Tabatha.

"So what happened, did he tell her to go?" asked Maggie.

"No, in fact he didn't even ask the question Heather was expecting. Instead, he told the group that he was going to talk to each of them for a few minutes to find out a little bit about them, and if they had a legitimate reason to be excused, he would consider it.

"Since Heather didn't think she had a legitimate enough reason, she sat quietly waiting for her name to be called. While she waited, Heather heard almost every person offer up their excuse and watched the judge deny each of them. When he finally called Heather up to the bench, he talked to her for a bit and then asked if there was a reason why she could not serve on the upcoming murder trial—which, by the way, she told me was supposed to last from four to six weeks."

"Heather should have told him about your brother-in-law's job!" volunteered Tricia.

"Oh yeah, good thought, except that lots of the people before her had tried the same excuse. Anyway, Heather told him that she really didn't have a legitimate excuse.

Then she went on to ask the judge if he wouldn't mind writing a note for her, though, to give to her hairdresser explaining why she had to cancel her appointment and ask to fit her in somewhere else."

"Oh my gosh, really? She actually said that?" asked Sarah.

"Yes, but the real shocker was the judge's response," said Tabatha.

"What did he say?" jumped in Tricia.

"Well first he asked whether he had heard her right and whether she was actually talking about her hairdresser. When Heather said yes, the attorneys and court people all busted out laughing and then quickly quieted down and just stared at her as if to say 'Ohhhh, you're in trouble now.'

"But the judge just continued to ask Heather questions. 'So I'm assuming your hairdresser is always busy because they're so good, is that right?' and then she answered, 'Yes, Your Honor, very good.' Then he said, 'I'm sure it would be very difficult for you to get another appointment, and it probably would take a long time, is that correct?' And she said, 'Yes, Your Honor, it would take a very long time.' Then the judge said, 'I'm thinking that would be a hardship for you, is that correct?' And Heather said, 'Yes, Your Honor, it would be,' and then Heather told me that the judge just picked up his hammer, I mean gavel, and banged it down on the bench, looked Heather in the eye and said, 'You're dismissed,'" said Tabatha.

"Wow, I can't believe it. Then what happened?" asked Sarah.

"Heather said the judge told her to meet the court officer in the back of the room. When she got there, Heather asked if she was supposed to go back downstairs to the sitting room and wait for them to call her again for another case, like the rest of the people had to do. But the officer just said, 'Nope,' and explained that the judge had dismissed her completely so she was free to go. Then Heather ran out of there as fast as possible." Tabatha laughed.

"Well that sure is funny—not to mention a perfect story for Thankful Thursday," said Sarah.

CHAPTER 20

Life's a Celebration!

"OH MY GOSH, she's adorable. Congratulations!" Sarah leaned over and put a small package on the bed. "Here's a little something for the two of you, I mean the three of you."

"Thanks, guys," said Paul.

"How are you feeling, Tricia?" asked Tommy.

"I'm great, Tommy, just a little tired," answered Tricia.

"Well she sure is beautiful. What did you name her?" asked Sarah.

"Samantha Lynn Evans," said Paul proudly.

Just then, the door opened and in marched the rest of the Decorating Club members all carrying an assortment of flowers, balloons and gifts.

"It's really nice of you guys to all come by," said Tricia humbly.

"Are you kidding? We wouldn't have missed it for anything. Besides, we figured the proud Papa's gotta be handing out cigars," joked Eric.

"As a matter of fact, I do have cigars for you."

Paul picked up the cardboard box from the hospital nightstand, opened it and began passing around the long cigar shaped chocolate wrapped in pink foil.

"Oh, these are so cute," said Maggie as she looked into the box. "I'm not going to eat it, but I want to take one anyway."

"Maggie, I had to do a double take when I saw you walk in. You really look fantastic!" said Tricia.

"Yeah, Maggie, you look great!" said Tommy.

"You can't still be on a diet, are you?" asked Jackie.

"Actually, I like to look at it more as a lifestyle than a diet," said Maggie.

"Would you believe my lovely lady here is back to the weight she was in high school," said Mark proudly.

"Good for you, Maggie," said Brittany.

"Ha ha, for every pound you've lost I'm sure I've put on three. It's a good thing we didn't start your house, Reshma, until I had this baby, because I was so big I wouldn't have fit in it! Not to mention been able to help," laughed Tricia.

"Oh, Tricia." Reshma giggled. "You couldn't have been that big. Besides, Anil and I are in no rush. We can wait until you're ready."

"Speaking of houses—" Eric moved over by Steve and patted his belly "—looks like someone needs to hit the gym."

"Very funny. No, I think I just need to cut down on all the scones and clotted cream!" protested Steve.

"Oh yeah, Jackie, how is everything going with your business?" asked Paul.

"Great! Honestly, I'm also glad we've had this time off because I'm so busy. I always knew that June and October were considered the busy months for weddings, but right now I have at least one booking every month for the next six months!"

"Wow, that's great, Jackie! Tommy and I have some friends whose niece just got engaged, and we gave them your number. I know she'll be calling you because she wants something very different and unique," said Sarah.

"Oh, that's great, thank you!"

"So, Paul, Mother's Day is coming. Have you made any plans yet?" asked Jackie.

"Umm, no, I haven't even thought of that," confessed Paul.

"Well you better start, buddy," chimed in Steve.

"Oh please," said Jackie as she glared over at Steve.

"Why, what happened, did you actually forget Mother's Day one year, Steve?" asked Brittany.

"Well, not exactly. It was after our first child was born and I asked Jackie what she'd like to do to celebrate. She told me we didn't have to do anything and she would be happy just working in her garden."

"OOOh, and you believed her?" asked Eric.

"Yeah, not one of my proudest moments. But, in my defense, back then, I was still in dental school and things were pretty tight. So when she said she really didn't want to do anything, I figured it must not be that big of a deal to her, and besides, she probably didn't want us to spend the money."

"Well that wasn't the only reason," interrupted Jackie. "I didn't want you to ask me what I wanted to do; I wanted you to think enough to plan it out on your own!"

"So what happened?" asked Anil.

"Nothing," said Steve.

"That's right, nothing!" said Jackie. "Absolutely nothing—not even a card."

"Oooh, bad move, buddy!" added Tommy.

"Well remember Mother's Day is around the corner, guys. Let's not make that mistake. I'd hate to see you all sleeping out in the dog house." Tabatha laughed.

"Yeah, that won't ever happen again," said Steve under his breath.

CHAPTER 21

Personal Stick Figures

"SO YOU WOULD buy three pink and one blue charm," explained the woman at the jewelry counter.

"But how will she know which one is me?" asked Katie.

"Well you would be one of the pink ones," said the sales woman.

"Yes, but which one?" asked Katie.

"Katie, the point is Mommy would have three girl stick figure charms and one boy to represent the four of you. Stick figures only represent the gender; they don't identify more than that. You would be one of the girl ones," said Tommy.

"But, Daddy, I don't like that. I want Mommy to be able to say, 'This one is Katie.'"

"Yeah, Dad, I want her to be able to point to the one that is the oldest and most creative and say that's me," added Maddie.

"And I want her to know which one is the smartest one!" said Darcy.

Just then Maddie pushed Darcy into the glass jewelry case and yelled, "Darcy, you're a jerk!"

"Dad, did you see that? Maddie just pushed me!" said Darcy.

"Girls! Settle down! Let's not forget why we're here. You've been arguing over what to get Mommy for weeks, and now we're out of time. Mother's Day is tomorrow," said Tommy impatiently.

"Well I think Mom's jewelry should represent all of us. But if it's just stick figures with pink and blue stones, it's not going to be any different from Mom's friend's necklaces. I think ours should represent who we are and what we like to do," said Darcy.

"Yeah, I agree with Darcy, Daddy," said Katie.

"I don't see what the big deal is," said Collin.

"That's because you're the only boy and there's only one charm to represent you," said Maddie.

"Well, kids, what do you want to do?" asked Tommy.

"I have an idea. Dad, can you take us to the grocery store and give us a bunch of quarters like Mom always does? Then we can get charms out of the machine, and we'll pick the ones that best represent us and turn them into our own necklace for her," said Maddie.

"Yeah, that's a cool idea. I wish I'd thought of it," said Darcy.

"Hmm, I know they have an ice cream charm. If we put that on, I know she's definitely going to know that one's me," said Katie excitedly.

With the clock winding down to zero, Tommy reluctantly agreed and then surmised, "It's got to be better than last year's macaroni necklace."

Happy Motoring Day!

"Look, Mommy, even the gas station put out a sign for you on your special day," said Katie.

"They did? What do you mean, Katie?"

"The sign over there... over there. See it; it says Happy Mother's Day!"

"No it doesn't. It says Happy Motoring Day. Can't you read?" said Darcy.

"Darcy, that's mean, please apologize to Katie," said Sarah.

"I'm sorry," said Darcy.

"Hey, Mom, are you sure you like our gift?" asked Maddie.

"Yes, Maddie, of course I do. Why do you ask?" asked Sarah.

"Well, it's just that we thought the charms would better represent us, but we didn't have as many choices as we thought we would," said Maddie.

"Yeah, I think Daddy is a cheapmater," said Katie.

"A cheapmater. What the heck is that?" asked Collin.

"You know, someone who doesn't give you enough quarters," said Katie.

"You mean a cheapskate," clarified Sarah.

"Yeah, that's what I mean, Daddy is a cheapskate. I'm sure if we had more quarters we would have gotten ones that were better," said Katie.

"Hey, I am in the car you know; I can hear you. Besides, I tried my hardest, but the store was getting ready to close," said Tommy.

"Listen, guys, I have an idea; I have a friend whose daughter works for a charm company in New York. If you want, maybe we can order some new charms that you feel represent you better and then make a whole new necklace. What do you think?" asked Sarah.

"I think it's a great idea because I hate cats," said Darcy.

"But the charm that stands for you is a cat, honey. I'm confused," said Sarah.

"See, that's what I mean! I couldn't get a dog charm, so I picked the cat because my friend Angela has a cat and I was hoping you would know that was me," said Darcy.

"Ha ha, that's adorable. Well hopefully we'll find a charm that you'll be happy with," said Sarah.

CHAPTER 22

Forgiveness

Project #6 - Reshma

Where am I?

THE STORY BEHIND the next and possibly final project for the Decorating Club members would prove to be quite different from the rest.

Although they had been living there for almost three years, Sarah's first impression upon entering the home belonging to Anil and Reshma Patel was that it looked more like two weeks!

"Welcome, it's so good to see you all," said Reshma as she opened the door and invited the girls in. "Please follow me into the kitchen, I have coffee on. But watch your step," she cautioned.

The floor of the living room was covered with a wide array of toys that continued to stream down the hall and into the kitchen. As the girls assembled, they each were handed a cup of coffee and directed to help themselves to a selection of snacks on the kitchen table.

"There's Ritz Crackers, Goldfish, Planters Peanuts and Jif, so please help yourself," encouraged Reshma.

"Wow, that's some combination. Is that what people eat in India?" Tricia jokingly asked.

"Oh no, not at all, but since we are here in America, I wanted to provide you with American goodies," replied Reshma.

"Thank you, Reshma," said Sarah, touched by Reshma's caring manner, "and since we're on the topic, I was wondering if you'd also share some of the other differences between our countries. I'm always fascinated by other cultures and traditions."

"Sure, well there are many differences, but in my mind one of the biggest is that India is a very collectivist society, while the US is comparatively more individualistic. In India, for instance, your family traditionally has a strong role in deciding who you plan to marry, and that leads to many arranged marriages instead of love marriages," Reshma shared.

"Wow, was your marriage arranged?" asked Brittany.

"No, mine was a love marriage, but my sister's marriage was arranged. When Divya turned twenty-two, she married a man ten years older than her. They had never met before that day—and while he's a good man and the families continue to feel it's a perfect match, Divya doesn't love him."

"Oh, wow, that's a shame. Is that why your family didn't arrange your marriage?" Maggie asked.

"No, that is not why," Reshma replied softly. "As a young girl, I dreamt of one day marrying for love. I would spend all my free time painting pictures of beautiful Indian brides who were in love. I always hoped that would be me one day. But, my parents wanted me to go to university to get a more marketable career. My father would tell me, 'Silly girl, stop painting those women with googly eyes and find an education that will make you look more attractive to future suitors!'"

"So how did you meet Anil? Was he from your country?" Maggie pressed.

"Oh no . . ." Reshma giggled before continuing, ". . . he's originally from New York, and I met him after I convinced my parents to let me take an au pair job in America. The plan was for me to visit the US for a year while on a J-1 visa. I would take some classes at the local college and then go back home to finish my schooling. They weren't very excited about it but finally agreed.

"My host family was a nice couple with two little boys, Anthony and Michael. They lived on a quiet street in Clifton, a district of Cincinnati, Ohio. Anthony's best friend was William, who lived three doors down and who just happened to have an older sister my age. Her name is Lilly, and it wasn't long before we became best friends.

"Lilly and I both attended the University of Cincinnati, although we weren't in any classes together. But, she was always telling me about a cute boy she knew from one of her study groups, how handsome he was as well as how he always made her laugh. It was Anil, and Lilly thought we'd make the perfect couple. I finally agreed to meet him and we started dating. Lilly was right, Anil was both handsome and funny as well as a good and caring man. It wasn't long before we both fell in love.

"Later, when Anil passed out, he was offered a job by the NCR Corp, but that meant he would have to move to their headquarters in Duluth, Georgia."

"Wait, what did you say... he passed out?" interrupted Tricia.

"Yes, oh, I'm sorry. I try very hard to speak good American English, but sometimes I slip. In my country that means he graduated," Reshma said in an apologetic way.

The girls all smiled and giggled, and then Sarah said, "Don't apologize, Reshma, you speak very well. Now please continue."

"Okay, thank you, Sarah. Well, anyway, his job opportunity would require Anil to relocate, and my visa was due to expire around the same time. That meant I would have to go back home to India.

"Neither of us wanted me to leave. Then one night while we were at dinner Anil suddenly got down on one knee and asked me to marry him," Reshma said with a smile, "and so we moved to Georgia together."

"So you never went back home?"

"Were your parents upset?"

"Did you just renew your visa?"

"Did your family come for the wedding?"

"Do you miss home?"

... The girls excitedly asked.

"No, I never went back home, and, yes, my parents were very upset with me. Unbeknownst to me, my father had actually been in the process of finalizing an arranged marriage for me. In fact, they were about to ask me to fly home and be married to the man they picked to be my husband. So, they were very angry and embarrassed when I told them I was marrying an American and staying here in America.

"No, thankfully I didn't need to renew my visa. It was for one year plus one month, and by then we already were married," explained Reshma.

"Phew, that's good, so you did not have to go back to India?" asked Maggie.

"Yes, Maggie, that is correct. Thankfully, the program I was under didn't include a requirement for me to return to my country after completion. I was able to get a green card because Anil was a US citizen. But in order to become naturalized, I had to pass a civics and English test."

"So did you ever go back to college?" asked Brittany.

"No, I have thought about it, but right now I am very busy taking care of Anil and baby Lilly," said Reshma.

"Oh, that's right, how sweet," said Sarah. "That's where Lilly got her name, after your matchmaker friend."

"Yes!" Reshma said proudly.

"But, Reshma, what about when Lilly is sleeping and Anil is working?" inquired Tricia. "What do you do then?"

"Well, I read, watch television, and spend my time becoming more familiar with the American lifestyle. The things I didn't necessarily learn while at university or studying for my citizenship tests. But, I haven't abandoned my art altogether. I like to draw pictures of all the products I see on TV. That's another big difference between here and back home. When I was growing up in

India there were not as many different product brands in the marketplace. As a result, I became fascinated with all the logos and images on the American merchandise, and I decided to draw them."

Reshma then picked up a small book from the counter and passed it to the girls. Inside were tons of realistic pictures of well-known food products including potato chip bags, soda cans, whipped cream containers, pickle jars and cereal boxes.

"Wow, these are great. You are very talented, Reshma!" Jackie declared. "Have you ever considered taking formal lessons? I think Anne Arundel Community College might offer a few courses you would enjoy."

"No, I'm not an artist, but thank you. I just taught myself how to paint pictures of brides as a child, and now I taught myself how to paint pictures of food instead," insisted Reshma.

"But that is art. It's known as pop art, and who knows, maybe you'll be the next Andy Warhol!" declared Brittany.

"Who?" said Reshma.

"He was an American artist and a leading figure in the visual art movement, also known as pop art. But, you could take your artistic talents in many different directions. Like maybe paint landscapes, everybody likes them," offered Tricia.

"Did you ever think of drawing portraits? I know someone looking to have pictures of their whole family done," said Maggie.

"That's a good idea. I can see if any of my clients would like to have wedding portraits done, if you'd like—especially since you started by drawing brides," offered Jackie.

"Oh no, thank you, but I no longer want to draw pictures of brides. That was in my past, when I was in India, but I live here in this country now," stressed Reshma.

"That may be true, Reshma, but that doesn't mean you have to stop being who you are. When I look around your house, I only see Lilly's toys and some of Anil's accomplishments and interests. But, there doesn't seem to be anything about you, your interests, your artistic talent or even your family heritage or culture. Just because you live here now doesn't mean you need to ignore where you came from or stop doing and sharing the things you're passionate about," said Sarah. "It's important for you to be the person you were made to be, and for your daughter, Lilly, and everyone else to know who that person is. Besides, it's clear that drawing is one of your gifts."

"Yeah Reshma, Sarah's right. I don't want to hurt your feelings but I don't see the *you* part of your story in your house," said Tricia.

"I agree… and besides you're so talented you can't keep that hidden in a box, Reshma you need to share it with the world!" offered Brittany.

"The world?? How do I do that?" asked Reshma

"Come on Reshma you already know the answer – You need to start from where you are," said Jackie.

"Well, where I am, is in America," stated Reshma.

"Yes you are physically here but I agree with Sarah you need to open up your shell and let the real Reshma out," said Tabatha.

"Yeah Reshma then we could help you tell the story of *all* the people who live here." said Maggie.

After a few moments of silently staring off into space, Reshma turned to them and somberly said. "Well my friends you have given me a lot to think about. I wish very much to have you help me tell my story. But first; I guess I need to go back and revisit where my story starts!"

Where am I going?

Later that day, Reshma put Lilly down for a nap, and for the first time in many years, made herself a cup of tea. Ever since she came to America Reshma had been drinking coffee, even though it wasn't something she particularly liked. In fact, her only reason for drinking it was to fit into the American lifestyle.

As Reshma sipped her tea, she thought about what Sarah and the other members had to say.

"Hmm, it's like I'm living a lie. I've turned my back on where I've come from and who I am. The truth is, I miss my family very much and want nothing more than to have them back in my life. I wonder if they want the same and whether they could ever forgive me."

Reshma nervously ran her hand around the sides of her cup as she tried visualizing what her parents' reaction might be.

Then just before dinner, Reshma finally got up the courage and made a long-distance phone call.

* * *

THE DECORATING CLUB

The Power of Tea

There's nothing like a warm cup of tea,
To settle your insides and offer clarity.
For some, the respite is a welcome relief,
For others, magic and potion is their belief
Yet, it doesn't really matter if you're young or old,
Look to the future, or drink it just because it's bold
Tea, affirmed for its power to heal the present,
Can also miraculously erase the past,
No matter how unpleasant.

How am I going to get there?

"Anil! Anil!" screamed Reshma.

"What is it, Reshma? What is it? What's the matter?" answered Anil.

"Nothing! That's the point, Anil! Nothing is the matter. Everything is great! Mummy and Papa are coming here to visit!"

"Wow, that's wonderful, Reshma! I'm so happy for you! That's great news! Hmm, I hope they like me," said Anil nervously.

"Of course they'll like you. Why wouldn't they?" said Reshma.

"Well it's because of me that you stayed and didn't marry that other guy. By the way, Reshma, how tall exactly is your father? Is he a big man?"

"No, he's not that big, just normal size. Why do you ask?"

"Oh, never mind, I was just curious," said Anil in a relieved tone.

"So when are they coming?" asked Anil.

"I'm not sure yet, but I know it's going to be very soon because Papa said he's going right out to buy the tickets. They said they would call me tomorrow with the details."

"Well I guess you girls will have to put our Decorating Club project on hold then, until after your parents leave," said Anil.

"Oh no, Anil, I forgot. I can't let Mummy and Papa see the house looking like this. It is storyless! What am I going to do?" asked Reshma.

"What do you mean it's storyless?"

"I don't know it just is. I don't have time to explain it I need to call Sarah right away!"

* * *

"Wow, Reshma, these pastries are delicious and so is this tea. What is it?"

"Oh, thank you, Maggie. They are traditional snacks from my country. The pastries are called samosas, and the drink is called chai," said Reshma, beaming with pride.

"Chai is a very good drink for the hot climate due to its cooling effect. Where I grew up in Bombay, chai is made very strong, and most people drink only a half cup, that is known as 'cutting chai.'

"Did you say cutting?" asked Maggie

"Yes cutting, I used to love watching the street vendors perform this; it's really quite fascinating.

"They start with a full cup of hot Chai and pour it into another cup from a height of almost three feet. They repeat the process back and forth until the Chai has cooled to a desirable temperature, and somehow, they never spill a drop. Often the cups are made of clay, and once the drink is finished, they are just smashed," Reshma explained.

"That is so cool. Reshma, do you have a recipe that you can share for the chai?"

"Yes, Maggie, and I'd be happy to."

"Awesome! Thanks, Reshma."

"I also want to tell all of you how much I appreciate you coming back over here today.

"Well I think I speak for all of us when I say we are so happy to hear that your parents are coming for a visit and of course want to help you however we can," said Sarah.

"Yeah Reshma that's so exciting, I bet you can't wait to see them," said Jackie.

"Were they surprised you called?" asked Brittany.

"Oh yes, they were very surprised and I was very nervous. But, I realized how much I miss them and how much I want them back in my life.

Jackie you were right, I needed to start where I was and for me that meant I needed to forgive my family and I needed to ask them to forgive me.

THE DECORATING CLUB

My concern now is that all of you were right and it might be hurtful to them if they don't see any of me or my heritage represented here.

So I am very hopeful that you can help me make it into a home that tells the story of Anil, Lilly *and* Reshma Patel," pleaded Reshma.

The girls happily agreed, sketched out a quick plan of attack and then busily got to work. First, they collected all of Lilly's toys and carried them down to the basement—now labeled the "Playroom."

Next, they took most of Anil's collection of outside interests including work-related recognitions, swimming trophies and all of his many books on photography and stylishly arranged them in his office.

"What about you, Reshma? What do you have from back home that we could incorporate into the décor?" asked Sarah.

"Sadly, I do not have much, just this old photo album with pictures of my family and relatives." she said nervously.

"I have an idea," said Tricia. "Sarah, why don't we turn the study into an art studio for her? We can take a lot of the photos from her album and get them framed, you know, of family and friends. Then hang them on the wall mixed right in with Reshma's art and pictures of her life with Anil and Lilly.

"Reshma, you can ask your sign guy to come over and paint something like Reshma's Living Wall or My Life—I don't know, but I do know somebody who writes creative advertising copy who might be able to help you think of something appropriate," she teased.

"That's a great idea!" Sarah replied.

"Yes, I like that very much, and that will also show my papa that I actually can paint things other than googly-eyed girls," Reshma proudly declared. "I am concerned, though, it's been a very long time since I've seen them, and I'm not sure what we will talk about. I am very excited, but to be honest, I'm also very nervous."

"I have an idea, how about a Decorating Club picnic? Everyone loves picnics. Besides, with all of us around it will help break the ice," offered Sarah.

"Yeah, Reshma, we can help you make Indian street food so your parents will feel at home," said Maggie.

"And we can have the guys flip some burgers so they can taste our food, too, if they'd like," suggested Jackie.

"I love the idea. That's very nice of all of you," said Reshma humbly.

"Perfect, we'll all plan to be here getting things ready when you and Anil go pick up your parents from the airport," said Sarah.

"Yup, sounds like a plan," said Tricia.

THE DECORATING CLUB

* * *

Reshma's parents boarded a plane in India, and approximately twenty-three hours later, after clearing customs, walked through the arrivals door at BWI airport and right into the arms of a beautiful woman, dressed in a traditional Indian Sari along with her matching baby girl. Standing next to them was Anil, nervously holding a colorful bouquet of flowers.

The day was filled with a lot of photo taking, a lot of laughs and a lot of tears, especially when Reshma took her papa inside to show him her living wall. There in front of him was a collage of pictures dating back to when she was a little girl right up to present day. Tears streamed from his eyes as he viewed one of Reshma's painted brides and beside it, a picture of her, all dressed in white, with the words "I married for love" underneath.

CHAPTER 23

Now What?

"GOOD EVENING, my name is Colleen. I'll be your server tonight."

"Hi, Colleen, I'm Tommy, and this is my beautiful wife, Sarah."

Colleen nervously smiled and then said, "Oh, hey, it's nice to meet you guys."

Colleen stood for a moment in front of the couple's table. It was clear that she wanted to say something but was left only with an awkward pause.

"I have to apologize because I was going to tell you the specials for tonight, but now I can't remember them," she nervously laughed.

"That's okay, we have that effect on people," fired back Tommy.

"We? Speak for yourself, buddy," teased Sarah.

"I've said them like a million times tonight, but I guess when you told me your names, it threw me off," admitted Colleen.

"I'm sorry," said Tommy, "force of habit."

"No! No, I mean I thought it was very nice. I have to say my name because I'm serving you, but no one ever tells me their names."

"Well, it's just our way of letting you know we appreciate your service," Tommy said humbly, "and besides, how can you tell everybody about the really cool couple you met tonight if you don't even know their names!" he teased.

"Ha ha, very true! Well I'll give you a moment to look over the menu, and then I'll be right back to tell you the specials and take your drink order," Colleen said as she excused herself.

"So, speaking of serving, it's been a couple months now since Reshma and Anil's project, and I was wondering what you and the Decorating Club have planned next. Will you be going back to work on new rooms in each of the member's homes? Or are you thinking of starting again with all new members? I know a lot of people have been asking me what's next."

"A lot of people have been asking you? My phone hasn't stopped ringing! Honestly, I don't have a plan. I mean, no! I'm not going to go back and help the girls take on more rooms. Really none of them has time for it now anyway, and as far as restarting the club with all new members, I don't know. Don't get me wrong, I'm so happy that I've had this opportunity, and I can't imagine where I'd be right now if it wasn't for the Decorating Club. But now I feel like God has a different plan for me—only I just don't know what it is yet," admitted Sarah.

"Well, I guess you'll just have to actively wait and listen," said Tommy.

"What do you mean by actively wait?" asked Sarah.

"Well, the way I see it there are two kinds of waiting. You can either passively wait or actively wait. If you passively wait, you're basically sitting there waiting for someone to tap you on the shoulder and say, 'Hey, you, do this.' But, when that doesn't happen or at least not in the time frame you might wish, you're more likely to give up and become frustrated or depressed. In which case you might force it and possibly go in the wrong direction. Or worse still, do nothing and just unplug from life a little more each day as you sit waiting for the answer."

"You mean kind of like what I did before?" asked Sarah.

"Exactly. But, by starting the Decorating Club and putting the needs of others in front of your own, you were a perfect example of actively waiting. In the process, you successfully shifted your focus and were able to share your gifts instinctively with your new friends."

"Okay, I'm back, and before I forget again, tonight's specials are: for an appetizer we have an amazing margherita flatbread with vine-ripened tomatoes, fresh mozzarella, tender basil, extra virgin olive oil and flaked with sea salt. Then we have stuffed chicken parmigiana. The chicken is sautéed and then stuffed with fresh basil and Italian cheeses and served over a delicious bed of Pasta Verde. My favorite tonight is the gorgonzola crusted beef medallions. They're served with a mushroom Marsala sauce, roasted vegetables and mashed potatoes.

"We also have a pan-seared salmon served with a limoncello glaze, fresh broccolini and roasted rosemary potatoes, and last but not least we have a traditional tiramisu that is out of this world. Phew, I did it!" Colleen said breathlessly.

"Wow that was a lot to remember. Thanks, Colleen, it all sounds great!" said Sarah.

"Okay, I'll give you guys another minute to think that over, but, Sarah, I have to ask you, where did you get that beautiful necklace. It reminds me of the old-fashioned charm bracelets women would wear filled with trinkets that represented the things they loved or were interested in," said Colleen.

"Oh, thank you. Yes, you're exactly right it is just like them. But my children made this one for me," answered Sarah.

"Wow, it looks so professional. I thought it came from a really nice store. I mean, how old are your kids?" asked Colleen.

Sarah laughed. "Well we have four, three girls and one boy. Our twins are the oldest; Maddie and Collin are twelve, Darcy is ten and Katie is seven."

"Oh my gosh, they're so young, and they made it for you?"

"Yes, it was all their idea for Mother's Day! They wanted me to have a necklace with personality, their personality." Sarah picked one of the charms on the necklace chain, "See this one?"

"Oh, it's an ice cream cone. I'm guessing you like ice cream, right?" asked Colleen.

"No. I mean, I do, who doesn't, but it's there to represent our youngest, Katie, who could eat it for every meal!" laughed Sarah.

"So you mean every charm represents them? What about all the glass hearts?" asked Colleen.

"Yes every charm represents them or an activity or adventure that we've shared together. See, this book is because Darcy and I went to meet her favorite author, and as far as all the hearts, they wanted to fill the rest up with their love," explained Sarah.

"Oh my gosh, that's beautiful. I love it! You guys should be so proud of them. They sound like really insightful kids," said Colleen before excusing herself from the table.

Tommy picked up a roll out of the basket and began buttering it.

"You know, Sarah, Colleen's actually right," said Tommy.

"What do you mean?" asked Sarah.

"Well you know the saying about how we learn by example?" asked Tommy.

"Yes," said Sarah.

"Well when I think about the kids' desire to have your necklace represent their passions and interests, I can't help but think about your philosophy of a house telling a story of the people who live there. Don't you see, it's the same thing—and that, my love, they learned from you," said Tommy.

Where am I?

Carefully carrying her coffee, Sarah entered their lodge-like family room and sat down in her favorite seat, an oversized leather chair. "Ah, I can't remember the last time I read this magazine, or any, for that matter," Sarah thought while picking up the Washingtonian, a premier magazine that highlights the "best" of Washington DC and the surrounding areas. As she flipped through the pages, something caught her eye. "Oh my gosh, it's Jackie!" she screamed. The title of the article was "This Is a Must—To Be Shared!"

"How clever, since the name of Jackie's custom bridal gown business is To Be Shared." thought Sarah? In the article, Jackie explains where her inspiration for the name of the business came from and what it means. She was quoted as saying, "I owe my success to my friend Sarah, who made me realize that we all have gifts and talents. Sometimes they just need to be taken out of storage and given a little dusting, before putting them back into use. She also taught me that everyone has a story to share, and that's what makes each of us unique.

"For instance, my story about how I met my husband began in a little café in the South of England," Jackie continued, "and with the help of Sarah and the rest of the girls from the Decorating Club, I was able to recreate and recapture the atmosphere of that restaurant in my home. It now serves as my office where I meet prospective clients."

"There we sit and enjoy some tea and scones while conversing about their unique story. Then I set out to design a couture gown that in some way incorporates a small symbol of their fairy tale. The representation is always placed on the outside of their dress—in plain sight, to be shared with the couple's guests—hence the name of my company." The article went on to call Jackie the fairy godmother of bridal gowns and finished with, "Forget about something borrowed or something blue, guests now want to hear the story of why you said I do."

"Oh my gosh, this is so cool. I'm so happy for her. I can't believe..."

Just then, Sarah's front door flew open and in ran Katie. "Mommy everyone is talking about Miss Maggie and you! They want to know when you're starting up the next Decorating Club. Everybody's mom wants to join!"

"Miss Maggie?" questioned Sarah.

"Yeah, she was interviewed on TV. They were asking her about her Zumba studio and talking to her about being some big shot for a juicing company now that she lost all of that weight."

Suddenly the door opened again, but this time with her middle child, Darcy, followed by Brittany's daughter, Elizabeth, and finally, Brittany.

"Mom, Mom, where are you?" screamed out Darcy

"I'm in the family room, Darcy, what's the matter?"

"Mom, can I sleep over at Elizabeth's house Saturday night and stay for the cool game they play on Sunday with strangers, please, please," begged Darcy.

Sarah smiled and then said, "Hi, Brittany, can you tell me what she's talking about?"

"Oh, she's talking about our new game: "If You Could Live Anywhere in the World, Where Would it Be and Why?"

"Each Sunday, we host a breakfast for those in need. Although the focus is more on the game than the food. We feel that it's a great way to expand our guests' and our children's minds and introduce them to places, things and possibilities they never thought attainable. As you might imagine, most of our guests have never lived anywhere else. The game is great because it introduces them to all sorts of options, and if they have a real desire to move and change their lives, we commit to helping them accomplish it.

"Sarah, you'd be very proud because we've also incorporated your formula of 'Where am I?' 'Where am I going?' and 'How am I going to get there?' to help them.

It's been very rewarding, and I have to say, David, the children and I have never been happier.

"We'd love to have Darcy join us, but she'll need to bring a sleeping bag, 'cause the house is still empty," Brittany added with a wink and a smile.

"Hmm, yet another example of living life in 3D?" Sarah mused to herself as they left.

CHAPTER 24

I'm Here...for Now

RING... RING... RING.

... "Hello? Yes, this is she."

... "Um, yes, it was my idea."

... "Excuse me, but who did you say this was again?"

... "Oh, okay, yes, it's nice to meet you too."

... "Well that's very nice, and I appreciate that, but I haven't yet decided on what's happening next, and so I don't know if it would make sense," said Sarah.

"I understand, Sarah, but our station is not as interested in what's next as it is in what has already happened," said the woman on the other end of the line. "You see, we like to spotlight local people who have done positive things right here in our own backyard, and well, to be honest, what you've done is very inspiring and very newsworthy to say the least, and we know our viewers would love to hear your story."

"Well, I'll think about it. But, it's not about me or what I've done. It's about what we all did together as a group. So the only way I'd even consider this is if you agree to interview all of the Decorating Club members together, and only if they also agree to be interviewed."

* * *

"Oh my gosh, I'm so nervous!" said Maggie as they all stood in a corner of the TV station lobby.

"Well, Maggie, at least you don't have to worry about television making you look ten pounds heavier any more. Instead it's me who has to worry!" said Tricia.

"Listen, you look great. Besides, it takes a good year to lose all the baby weight, at least that's the way it was for me with each of my kids," said Jackie.

"A year? Ugh!" said Tricia.

The girls' conversation abruptly ceased as their attention quickly shifted to the attractive woman now approaching them.

"Welcome, ladies, I'm so glad you decided to join me today. I'm Leticia Jones. I hope I haven't left you waiting too long."

"No, we just got here. Hi, I'm Sarah, and this is Jackie, Maggie, Brittany, Tricia, Tabatha and Reshma," Sarah said as she waved her hand around while introducing each of the girls.

"Well I appreciate you all coming here today, and I'm so excited to hear your story. Would you please follow me so we can get started?"

The girls followed Leticia down a dark hallway and into the brightly lit studio room.

"Wow, this looks just like someone's living room," commented Reshma.

"Please make yourselves comfortable," said Leticia.

Once everyone was seated, she began, "Okay, so the first thing I'd like all of you to do is just relax and be yourselves. There's nothing to be nervous about. Like Reshma said, we're just going to pretend this is my living room, and we're all just sitting here talking. But first, I'm going to ask you to give me just a few more minutes to skim over my notes, and then we'll begin."

"Sure, Leticia, take all the time you need," said Sarah.

"Yes, take your time—I mean a lot of time. I'm waiting for my nerves to calm down," joked Tricia.

Once Leticia finished looking over her notes, she gave Joe the cameraman the heads up and he began counting down.

"Five . . . four . . . three . . . two . . . one."

"Good afternoon, this is Leticia Jones. Today, I bring you a very special story of some neighbors who live right here in Anne Arundel County. Together they formed the Decorating Club, working side by side helping to redesign each other's homes. One of the things that makes this story so exceptional is that it's a wonderful example of women helping and supporting one another. But, where this story took a turn is when the primary focus shifted from redesigning their homes to redesigning their lives.

"Now please join me in welcoming Sarah Durham, whose idea it was to create the Decorating Club. Sarah, I've heard of all kinds of clubs, but this is the first time I've ever heard of a decorating club. Could you tell us how you came up with the idea?" said Leticia.

"Well to be honest, it was quite unexpected, and I actually was kind of hoping it would never happen," said Sarah.

"Never happen? I don't understand. Why would you suggest it if you didn't want it to happen?" questioned Leticia.

"It was the best alternative I could think of at the time. You see, I had a design business back in New Jersey, but after we moved here, I wasn't sure I wanted to restart it again in Maryland, at least not at that particular moment. But, when we first met and the girls came to my home and learned of my background, they asked if I would consider taking all of them on as clients. Since I wasn't ready for that, I countered with an offer to help them for free," said Sarah.

"And you really thought they would pass on your free offer?" asked Leticia.

"Yes, I mean have you ever gone to the book store and spent an hour going over all the recipes in the book before deciding to purchase it only to then go home and never make one recipe?" said Sarah.

"Ha ha, yes I have," said Leticia.

"Well that's pretty much what I was hoping for," said Sarah.

"But instead we all jumped on it!" Jackie laughed.

"Yes, but it wasn't exactly a free lunch," added Tabatha.

"It wasn't? Please tell us what you mean by that, Tabatha," said Leticia.

"Well, Sarah made us all vow to roll up our sleeves and work alongside her," said Tabatha.

"Vow? You mean formal like?" asked Leticia.

"Yes! Beyond formal! We even have our own membership cards," Tricia laughed. "No offense, Sarah, but at first, we did think it was all a bit much. We even worried that you'd be making us a special club handshake," said Tricia kiddingly.

Leticia giggled as she put her hand over her mouth trying to disguise her smile.

"Okay, so when Sarah told you she would help for free, she wasn't saying she would just do it all, but instead said you'd have to help. Do I have that right?" said Leticia.

"Yes, that's right," said Reshma.

"Okay, so that's still a great offer, isn't it?" asked Leticia.

"Oh, let me answer that one," said Brittany.

"Sure, go ahead, Brittany," said Leticia.

"Okay, well it's no secret, but up to that point I was the only one out of the group that had any experience in designing—I mean, except for Sarah, of course," began Brittany.

"Excuse me, but exactly what experience did you have over all of us when we started?" asked Tricia.

"Well, I know a thing or two about quality decorating, but anyway, what I was going to say is we didn't actually think she was going to make us do the manual labor," said Brittany.

Just then Sarah, who had been sitting quietly, listening, smirked and said, "That's exactly why I wanted you all to swear to the terms!"

"Ha ha, you know we're only messing with you, right, Sarah? After all, I was the one who was the biggest pain in the butt. I'm sure you all wanted to kill me most of the time," said Tricia.

"No we didn't!" said Reshma.

THE DECORATING CLUB

"Yes we did!" said Brittany

"Umm, yeah, I'm afraid she's right," said Jackie.

"Sorry, honey, but, yes, we did," said Maggie.

"Tricia, you were just in pain back then," offered Tabatha.

"Oh, do you mind sharing with us why you were hurting, Tricia?" asked Leticia.

"No, not at all. I guess simply put, I had become a poster child for fear. I was stuck in a job I hated and my relationships were suffering all because I was too afraid to do anything about it. Yet what I learned was nobody could fix it for me. I had to take ownership of my own life. Looking back, I guess that's why Sarah insisted we all take ownership of our own decorating projects too. I mean, after all, how can anyone help you if you yourself don't know what you want?" said Tricia.

"Wow, that's well said, Tricia. I think you're right. I know I for one have been guilty of that, especially with my home. Instead of taking more of an interest I've hidden behind saying, 'I'm not talented, so I've just copied what others have done,' and while it looks pretty inside, it's not me, and I just don't feel comfortable," said Leticia before looking back down at her notes.

"Okay, let's talk color wheel, Tricia. What would you say was the predominant color or colors used in redesigning your home?" asked Leticia.

Tricia smiled as she looked at all the other members, and then in unison the team yelled out, "PINK!"

"Now I'd like to address my next question or should I say comment to Tabatha. Tabatha, I understand the members helped you and your husband launch a new business, a vegan health bar, to which I say to all of you 'I am eternally grateful!'" Just then, Leticia pulled out a half-eaten bar from her pocket and held it up to the camera.

"These Tab Bars are the most delicious snack bar I have ever eaten. They are filled with nothing but all-natural ingredients and are very low in calories. And the best part is you can now find them on the shelves in all the health food stores in the area."

"Thank you, that's very kind of you to say, and I'm so happy you're enjoying them," said Tabatha.

"So, Tabatha, would you please share how the Decorating Club helped you and your husband," asked Leticia.

"Sure. It's actually kind of crazy how it all came about. The concept was literally birthed at the impending closing of a door. See, at the time, my husband was considering retiring, and I was concerned what that might look like. I mean, sure, it also meant my life would change quite a bit with him home all the time. But, my main concern was for him. He has excelled at his job and has always remained very active. So, I worried that if he just unplugged he would feel like his purpose had dried up.

"The bottom line is he had always dreamed of one day creating his own health food line and while he's known for repeating his mantra— 'If you need to turn a tanker it's important to start early'—I convinced him that there's no time like the present," said Tabatha.

"That's so wonderful!" exclaimed Leticia. "Oh, and I'd just like to add that I think a chocolate banana Tab Bar could be a winner, especially for those who might like that combination as much as I do," she said with a wink.

"Now let's go back to you, Brittany. I've been told that you have a huge beautiful mansion. It must have taken a long time to work on your home and fill all of those rooms," said Leticia.

The stage filled with laughter, squeaks and shrills as the girls all reacted to Leticia's last comment.

"What? What did I miss? What's so funny?" asked Leticia.

After what seemed like forever the roaring laughter finally settled down and Brittany began to speak, "The question is not how many rooms we filled, but how many we emptied. And to that I say, all but one."

"Wow, I wasn't expecting that. Perhaps you'd like to expand on your answer?" questioned Leticia.

"I was guilty of putting value on all the wrong things. I became so caught up with trying to impress others that I began to lose the things most important to me. I'm embarrassed to say, I was a selfish, self-centered snob!" declared Brittany.

Not knowing what to say next, Leticia put her head down and nervously shuffled around her papers.

"Excuse me, Leticia, I'd like to jump in here if I may," said Sarah.

"Yes, by all means, please do, Sarah," said Leticia.

"I don't think the question is who Brittany was; I think the question is who Brittany is. Brittany is one of the most generous and compassionate people I know. Who now seeks not to be served but to serve," said Sarah.

"Thank you, Sarah. That means a lot," said Brittany humbly.

Staring into the camera Leticia continued, "Now some of you may have already read about the next member we are about to discuss in the Washingtonian Magazine. Jackie, I love the name of your bridal gown business and the notion behind it: To Be Shared. You are an inspiration to all the woman out there who have devoted their entire lives to their families and then were left feeling like what's next?"

"Thank you, Leticia. Yes, it's a horrible feeling to be left wondering if you even matter anymore. That's the way it was for me for a long time after my four kids flew the coop. But Sarah helped me see that I still had a lot to offer, and my friends here helped me turn it into a reality," said Jackie.

"I'm sure our audience is curious how exactly they did that, so could you please explain a little?" said Leticia.

"Well I'm a very visual learner, so when Sarah told me that there were a lot of empty nests around her house and yet she never saw one mother bird just sitting on them, well I think that finally got through to me. Then by actually filling out the questionnaires, I had the opportunity to focus on my interests and me for the first time in many years. Together we then went on to convert my kids' two unused bedrooms, one into a work studio and the other an office where I meet my clients," said Jackie.

"That's a wonderful success story, Jackie, and it makes me want to get married all over again. Only kidding if you're watching, honey," joked Leticia.

"Now I'm sure the next member's story was not the only life enhanced as a result of the club's collaboration, but instead, I have it on good authority that there are a lot of mothers and daughters in Anne Arundel County that are also benefitting from it. Maggie Cartwright and her daughter, Daniella, have started a Zumba studio in their home. With the help of the Decorating Club, including the club's newest members, the husbands, they were able to turn their unused basement into a gorgeous, novel place to sweat.

"The best part is, unlike any other traditional gym; the Zumba studio was created specifically to bridge and strengthen the relationship between mothers and daughters. Maggie, talk about spotting a need. Whoa, I think that was brilliant. I personally don't have any little ones yet, but I'm aware of the challenges others share, especially during the teenage years," said Leticia.

"Thank you, Leticia, but it would be one-sided of me to blame all my challenges on my daughter. The truth is I had given up on life. I felt my best years were behind me, and as a result, I made settling my middle name. I blamed my daughter and my husband for our relationships, when in the end it was me who needed to shoulder the blame," said Maggie.

"Wow, how incredibly honest of you. Thank you for sharing, Maggie, and please know you remain a brilliant example of someone determined to change what they no longer like," said Leticia.

"Reshma, Sarah shared her philosophy of a home telling a story. So what story does your home now tell?"

"My home was pretty much nondescript. It didn't really tell a story of my family or at least anything of me," said Reshma.

"Would you like to explain why you felt that way and what has now changed?" asked Leticia.

"I left my homeland and everything I knew and loved when I came to this country. Then I met my husband; we fell in love and married. My family was very upset with me because they expected me to honor family tradition and partake in an arranged marriage. They felt as if I turned my back on them, and in many ways, I did. I then tried very hard to fit into my new life and embrace the American way, but I found myself living a lie.

"After joining the Decorating Club and working alongside these ladies, I realized that I no longer wanted to run away from my past, but instead bring who and what I am into my current life. My home no longer mimics American or Indian homes. Instead, now every wall reflects the love I have for my family and the talents I've been blessed with," said Reshma.

"Thank you, Reshma. What a great reminder to all of us to be the person we were created to be," said Leticia.

"So I guess the next and final question is where does the club go from here? I address that question to you Sarah," said Leticia.

"Well, Leticia, I believe there's a time and season for everything. The Decorating Club came into existence when each of us in one way or another needed it. Let's face it, we as women are constantly putting the needs of others before our own. It's just a fact; I guess it's the way we've been wired.

"It's like being on a treadmill twenty four-seven. But, once that treadmill breaks down or our sneaker becomes untied, we're finally forced to stop. Then we're left wondering, where do we go from here? I guess the club has given each of us the opportunity to pause and take that long hard look into the mirror at our own circumstances.

"After we had a chance to identify where we were, we helped each other figure out where each of us wanted to go. The next part was much more fun, because that's when we worked together to create a roadmap and took action to reach our own individualized destinations.

"But where do we go from here? I think for right now each of us is where we are supposed to be. That's not to say that where we are is where we will remain forever. It's just like redesigning our homes. When our kids are small, we need that extra room to serve as a nursery. Then as they get older, the room best serves as a playroom. Then when they finally move out, we look back at the space. This time with two choices: Either hold onto the past and mourn days gone by, or we can take ownership. Maybe the room's best purpose now is to be a home gym or office for us to pursue our own dreams and aspirations.

"All I know is that I am truly grateful for having had the experience and hope it serves as an example and provides encouragement to others who may be questioning their own purpose," Sarah concluded.

"This is Leticia Jones; thank you for tuning in today and inviting us into your home. I'd also like to thank Sarah and the rest of the Decorating Club Members for sharing their inspiring story with us. And I leave you with a takeaway from today's interview: don't just buy the cookbook, but make the recipes: there's a lot of hungry people out there!"

"Well, Joe, it looks like that's a wrap!"

Afterword

> Be ye transformed by the renewing of your mind.—Romans 12:2

While there is a little bit of me in each of the Decorating Club members, three best reflect the challenges I encountered, unfortunately re-experienced and ultimately led me to writing this book.

In late August of 2013, I relocated back to the northeast with my husband; in some ways, we were retracing the steps of a similar trip made to Maryland in the month of August 12 years earlier. During the time between a lot had happened and a lot had changed, for everyone.

But for me, while excited about coming home again, the relocation brought with it the same unsettling feeling it had before; only this time it seemed more intense, and I believe it is because things were not the same as last time. This made even more challenging my dread of having to start over again in a new town where I knew no one and face the need to go through yet another time in my life when "me" was not really "me."

What had changed? Well, a few years earlier, we decided to close the small business that my children and I had successfully operated for eight years. At first, the business had seemed like a crazy idea to many, but to my husband and me it seemed like a logical next step.

The company, 3 sisters and a brother LLC ultimately operated two storefronts, The Bead Shack and Café Décor. The business soon became well known for serving the local community by fostering creativity for children and adults of all ages. There they learned how to make jewelry, earned scout badges, and celebrated birthdays and other social gatherings. At the time, our children were 12, 12, 10, and 7 and with my oversight as CEO, they ran all the business operations each day right after school, between and amongst sports and their other activities. I generally worked alone each day before school let out and then alongside the kids until closing. As the businesses grew we hired other children to work with us, and I enjoyed feeling as if we had an extended family.

It's very difficult for new businesses to make it through their first year, and many rarely make it past five. But, our company was able to remain in existence quite a while longer, and I believe it's all because we never viewed the business solely as an opportunity to make money. Instead, we viewed it as an opportunity for our children to learn life skills and make a difference in the lives of others. However, as time passed, it became obvious that it was time for the three sisters and a brother to pursue their own individualized dreams, leaving me with a huge void.

In life, everything has a season, and it was clear that ours had now come to an end. I knew it would come one day, but similar to Jackie, I still felt like an empty nester, in my case one on steroids since my kids hadn't just left home, they had also left my workplace!

Although, I really wasn't ready for what happened next.

"It's too bad you closed; I thought the kids would come back after they all graduated and run it."

"So, Sue, what do you have planned next?"

"You're so talented; I can't wait to see what you come up with."

These are just some of the questions and comments I received each day. While all well intended, for me they were just reminders of the cold hard reality. I was now an unemployed CEO, and while my children were all off pursuing their dreams, I found myself with no clear direction of my own and just the painfully lost feeling of missing my babies.

The days led into weeks and the weeks into months, and I found myself not one bit closer to uncovering my next steps. Yet it wasn't for lack of trying! Everyday I'd get up and reclaim my spot on the couch, where I would stay the entire day with my laptop trying to find answers to the burning question—what's next?

As that question was playing over and over in my mind, my thoughts were opening the door and allowing fear to walk right in. Some of it may have been caused by news coverage of local, national, and worldwide events or the incessant health-related marketing campaigns, as Tricia suggested can happen. But, most of my fear was simply about me not knowing what the future held in store and struggling to find my direction.

Like Sarah, questioning whether I still made a difference, I felt as though I had lost my sense of purpose. As I downloaded articles and books promising me that I would discover my purpose if I just followed their seven steps, instead of moving forward, I stood still. I even made it a point to watch celebrity commencement speeches thinking their words would be the gold I was searching for, but soon realized they weren't talking to me. In fact, no one was talking to me . . . How could they? They didn't know how I was feeling!

Finally, as I shared with you in the beginning of this book, it was when I remembered the special times I enjoyed with the members of the original Decorating Club that I was able to see my way forward. I remembered and renewed my concentration on doing the simple things that each of us already know instinctively, just by the way we feel when we do them. Things like being thankful, offering encouragement, focusing on the good, making a plan, helping someone, and sharing my own gifts and talents that enabled me once again to see more clearly the road ahead. Interestingly, they also had helped us shape the mission statement for our family business:

> *"Our greater purpose is to share our gifts and talents with others and encourage them to do the same."*

Thank you.
Susan M. Meyers

Recipes

I. TAB Bars

   Ingredients:

   Blueberry Chia Jam:
   - 1 ½ cups blueberry (frozen)
   - 1 ½ tbsp. chia seeds
   - 1 tbsp. pure maple syrup

   Bars
   - 1 cup oat flour
   - 1 cup old fashioned oats
   - 2 tbsp. coconut sugar (or brown sugar)
   - ½ tsp. cinnamon
   - ¼ tsp. salt
   - ½ tsp. baking soda
   - ½ cup unsweetened applesauce
   - ¼ cup pure maple syrup
   - ¼ cup coconut oil, melted
   - ¼ cup shredded coconut

Directions:

1. Preheat oven to 325. Grease an 8 x 8-inch baking dish with coconut oil or cooking spray.
2. Heat a small saucepan over medium heat. Add blueberries, chia seeds and maple syrup. Cook for about 10 minutes, stirring often. Use a potato masher to mash the blueberries for the "jam" layer. Set aside.
3. Combine oats, oat flour, sugar, cinnamon, salt, baking soda and shredded coconut in a large bowl.
4. Add applesauce, maple syrup and coconut oil, stirring to combine.
5. Set aside a heaping half cup of the oat mixture and then press the rest evenly into the prepared pan. Top with blueberry chia jam, spreading evenly with a spoon or spatula.
6. Sprinkle the rest of the oat mixture on top.
7. Bake for 30 minutes. Cool completely on a wire rack before cutting into 12 bars.
8. Store in the refrigerator.

II. Indian Masala Chai
(Serves 2-3 cups)

Ingredients:

- 4 whole cloves
- 2 cardamom pods
- 1-inch cinnamon stick—broken up
- 1-inch fresh ginger—cut up and mashed
- 6 peppercorns
- ½ tsp fennel seeds
- 3 cups water
- ½ cup milk
- 2 tbsp. sugar
- 2 tbsp. loose tea
- ¼ cup chopped fresh mint leaves

Directions:

1. Crush all the dry spices.
2. Add to the water, ginger and mint.
3. Bring to a boil and switch off heat.
4. Cover and steep for 15 minutes.
5. Add milk, sugar and tea.
6. Bring back to a boil and switch off heat.
7. Cover again and let steep for 5 minutes.
8. Strain and serve.

About the Author

Susan Meyers is an optimist who believes the world would be better served if everyone were more aligned with their greater purpose. The challenge as she sees it is not only to serve one's purpose but also to adapt as it changes from time to time.

While Susan has worn many hats throughout her life, serving as CEO of her children's business, *3 Sisters and a Brother, LLC* is the role of which she is most proud. It began in the family's basement when they were just 12, 12, 10, and 7 and soon expanded into two storefronts; within less than eight years, it became a well-known brand in the local community.

As time passed and each of the children began to take flight, Susan and her family made the decision to close the business. With each of her four children off pursuing their own individualized dreams and careers, Susan had to deal with a new title; unemployed CEO; as well as the closed doors that it represented for her more personally.

Finding herself questioning her own purpose and determined to regain it, Susan invested her time looking for answers. It soon became clear that none of the information she found talked to her concerns or even spoke the same language.

Eventually, Susan was reminded of what she already knew and in the hope of helping others facing similar challenges, was moved to write *The Decorating Club*.

Today, Susan makes her home with her husband and youngest daughter in Fairfield, CT. For more information, visit www.susanmmeyersauthor.com.

Thank you for reading my book!

I would greatly appreciate it if you leave a brief review and let me know what you think.

Notes:

CPSIA information can be obtained
at www.ICGtesting.com
Printed in the USA
FSHW011743260321
79792FS